PRAISE FOR EMPI BARYEH

Praise for Most Eligible Bachelor
"An engaging book that made me laugh, want to dance, and had me developing a crush on the hero." ~ Nana Prah, Author

"Best Book of the Year!" ~ 2017 Ufere Awards

Praise for Forest Girl
"This story is magical." ~ Goodreads reviewer

"The author managed to manoeuvre the ups and downs, surprises, twists and turns of this unusual relationship, keeping the reader in suspense till the end." ~ Celestine Nudanu

ALSO BY EMPI BARYEH

Chancing Faith
Most Eligible Bachelor
Forest Girl

Empi Baryeh

his
Inherited
PRINCESS

First Published in Great Britain in 2018 by
LOVE AFRICA PRESS
103 Reaver House, 12 East Street, Epsom KT17 1HX
www.loveafricapress.com

ISBN: 978-1-9164755-6-4
Also available as ebook

ACKNOWLEDGEMENT

A big thank you to Kiru Taye who (to my utmost frustration at the time) suggested we write the princesses stories first. You know what I mean.

A special thank you to MacDonald K. B. Simpson (Uncle Mac) for helping me with the Arabic translations that enabled me to unearth Omar's voice. *Shukran Jaziilan.*

Another special thank you to my friend, Naa Kwarley-Aba, for being my sounding board, cheerleader, and the first person aside from me to fall in love with Omar and India.

To my editor, Zee Monodee. You are fabulous to work with. As we say in Ghana, *ayekoo.*

Thank you to everyone who contributed in some way to bring Omar and India's story to life.

To my mother who told me a true story about an inherited widow, which sparked my desire to write a fictional one.

CHAPTER ONE

"I'm sorry, My Lady, but your husband...Prince Majid didn't make it."

Something is wrong with that sentence.

Princess India Saene couldn't figure out what, though. Her muddled thoughts made it difficult to piece anything together.

The wedding. It was the last thing she remembered. Her marriage to Majid marked the beginning of an alliance between her kingdom, Bagumi, and the Sahelian kingdom of Sudar. She'd only met her husband a month before their wedding, and although they weren't a love match, he'd been the perfect host, and she'd believed they could eventually grow to love each other.

"Where is he?" she asked.

Her tongue felt like a piece of parchment paper in her mouth, dry and tasteless...weighty. She barely managed to slit open her equally heavy eyelids before the bright lights above forced her to shut them again.

"Erm..."

Hesitation. She frowned, but before she could ask why, her mind produced another memory: she and Majid in a car—on their way to their honeymoon.

What did the woman mean by Prince Majid didn't make it? Was she alone at their honeymoon? Why would he not come with her? His coronation, scheduled for next week, gave them barely five days for this trip. Why would he miss even a day?

Perhaps something to do with his father, King Rafael, who had announced his abdication for medical reasons not too long ago. From the little she knew of Majid, she couldn't think of anything else that would cause him to abandon her without prior notice. A year ago, her father had suffered a mild heart attack, which had sparked debate about him handing over to her eldest brother. Luckily, he'd bounced back and had been cleared by the doctors to resume work full-time.

She'd understand if a situation with King Rafael had caused Majid to cut their honeymoon short. Or had he informed her, and she couldn't remember? Frustration mounted as her mind simply refused to yield to her demands for recollection.

"When is he returning?"

"My Lady, I don't have the authority to respond to that."

"What do you mean?"

She pried her eyes open again, blinking. Her mind drifted off as her surroundings became clearer. White ceiling, stark white walls, a constant beeping sound...*and that smell*. A woman's face came into focus; she wore a mask of concern.

Recognition poured into India's mind. "Salma?"

Her Sudari personal assistant smiled, relief taking over her features. "You recognised me. Thank God. They said you might not, which would be a bad sign."

"Where are we?"

"We're at the hospital."

"Hospital?" The beeping sound fit with this explanation, but why would she be in a hospital and not on her honeymoon? "When is Majid returning?"

At the look of discomfort on Salma's face, threads of worry wound tight around India's chest.

"Salma, would you please give me a moment with my wife?" a male voice spoke before she could express her concerns.

The voice vibrated through her, putting a kick in her chest and a sense of calm in her heart. Strange, she'd never realised how deep Majid's voice was. She remembered it as a gentle tenor, but he'd just spoken in a tone more bass than tenor, issuing words with the smoothness of a warm knife cutting through butter.

"Of course, Your Royal Highness," Salma said, curtseying.

India tried sitting up, and a sharp pain zinged through her head and body, causing her to wince and lie back down.

"No, My Lady," a third person said. A female who spoke with gentleness, belying an unmistakable authority in her delivery. "You mustn't move."

"How are you?"

Her husband's deep voice washed over her.

Yes, she could definitely grow to fall in love with that voice. He sounded so close. She turned slowly, meeting his dark brown stare.

Confusion made her blink. Twice. The face staring back at her wasn't Majid's.

"Omar?"

The deep, smooth-as-butter voice belonged to Omar?

The brothers had similar eyes but bore little resemblance beyond that. Majid carried his lean, six-foot frame with the grace of an athlete, whereas Omar stood at about five-eleven, his muscular body honed to perfection. Both had undergone military training, which probably explained their extremely fit physiques, but Omar oozed sexual charisma and a certain feral attractiveness that probably had countless woman falling at his feet.

Even she had experienced a moment of breathlessness when she'd met him briefly a month ago, but she'd known better than to put any stock in such a fleeting sensation, especially since their first meeting had also marked her betrothal to his brother.

Yet, for some inexplicable reason, her mind retrieved images of their first encounter. She and her father had been led into the room where King Rafael and Majid had been waiting. Soon after the introductions, a knock had sounded, and Omar had entered. His gaze had captured hers, and for several seconds, she'd forgotten to breathe. The same thing had happened only moments after when they'd been introduced and he'd taken her hand.

She pushed aside the thoughts, focusing on her present need for answers. What was Omar doing here? Had Majid sent him?

"Is she in a lot of pain, Doctor?" Omar asked, his gaze directed at someone on the other side of the bed.

"She shouldn't be in unbearable pain, Your Royal Highness. In fact, we've reduced the dosage of her pain medication."

"Why are they calling you Your Royal Highness?"

As she'd been made to understand, there were three formal styles used in addressing members of the royal family in Sudar. 'Majesty' for the king, 'Royal Highness' for the Queen and the heir apparent, and 'Highness' for everyone else.

"Wh—where's Majid?"

Her voice grated against her dry throat. Worry snaked up her spine. Something was wrong. She felt it in her bones.

Omar looked at her, and she found herself trapped in his gaze.

"How much do you remember?"

She frowned. "Remember?"

As if his rich voice had unlocked a door, it came to her all at once. She and Majid had been in the car, discussing the protocols to be observed for his coronation. Funny, since he'd apparently already broken one rule by travelling in the same car with her. She remembered the relief with which she'd latched on to the topic, glad to take her mind off how they'd approach their first night as husband and wife.

Then...

Bang!

It sounded like a gunshot or maybe a canon. The car careened to the left. Everything happened so fast. The driver swore, maintaining an iron grip on the steering wheel, but the car kept speeding.

"Watch out!" Majid yelled.

Screeching tires, then another *bang*! Something had hit them. She only remembered seeing headlights at the window before they were airborne. The car may have flipped over before crashing to the ground. Then, everything went black.

She shut her eyes as if it would somehow turn off the faucet of memories. Warmth engulfed her, and she realised Omar had taken her hand as he sat on the bed.

"You and Majid had an accident," he said softly.

"How's he?"

Dread clutched her gut, telling her she knew the answer. *Prince Majid didn't make it.*

"Majid fought bravely, but eventually succumbed to his injuries."

"No," she whispered, tears filling her eyes.

For several seconds, she hoped this was a nightmare. She'd wake up and find Majid lying by her side, and they'd laugh about this weird dream. Because if this wasn't happening in her head, then it meant Majid had died; she was a widow. What did it mean for the alliance between their two nations?

Her mind was in no position to process matters of such enormity. She refocused on what Omar had said.

One word stuck in her mind.

"Eventually? How long have I been here?"

"Two weeks," he answered. "Since you're awake now, you'll be coming home soon."

Coming home. Why did that sound off? She frowned as something else occurred.

"You called me your wife."

He stared at her for a long moment as though trying to decide whether to answer.

"In accordance with our tradition, I inherited my brother's widow."

"What?" She looked beyond him at Salma who nodded. "How could we be married if I've been here the past two weeks?"

"We observed the obligatory ten days of mourning, but after that, nothing stopped us from performing the widow inheritance rites."

Her heart pounded, fuelled by fury. "You can't marry me without my consent."

"I'm afraid the alliance between our kingdoms supersedes your consent. Or mine, for that matter. The only party who needed to be consulted was your king."

"My father agreed to this? Does he even know I'm in the hospital?"

He nodded. "Your parents and your brother, Azikiwe, arrived here the day after the accident. King

Ibrahim returned for the marriage ceremony, and I've kept your family updated on your progress."

She shook her head, unable to wrap her mind around his words. Had her father truly been a part of this?

"Sire," the other female, whom India deduced from the lab coat and stethoscope was the doctor, interrupted. "She needs rest."

Omar nodded, although his gaze remained on India.

He leaned in. Panic stole into her. Did he mean to kiss her? She couldn't allow him to do that as if any of what he'd said was okay with her. She'd committed herself to his brother, not to him. She willed herself to speak, or turn away, but his musky scent surrounded her, engulfed her senses, and her voice caught in her throat.

She held her breath as his lips touched her temple. A flame ignited from the spot, expanding over her as hot threads of pleasure and confusion, and for a moment, she forgot the pain in her body.

Pulling back, he stood. "Rest now, *ya jameel*. We'll talk soon."

In her battered state, her heart had no defence against his allure or the endearment—*my beautiful*—uttered with the ease of a man used to having women fall at his feet. She found the strength to look away, shamed to discover her response to him hadn't been as fleeting as she'd convinced herself.

"Can I have a private word with you, Doctor?" Omar said.

"Certainly, Sire."

India shut her eyes against Omar's retreating figure, the gesture releasing unshed tears. In the solace of her mind's eye, she sought to reject his declaration, reject him.

However, her mind veered off course, focusing on the heat from his kiss. Guilt slammed into her. Majid's kiss at their wedding had been sweet, but it hadn't packed the kind of heat Omar's lips had aroused.

What could it mean? She'd never been given to ephemeral emotions. Love and passion didn't have a place in marriages of alliance.

Her reaction to the kiss had to be nothing more than a result of her jumbled emotions, because falling for Omar had to be all kinds of wrong.

***

Several hours later, Prince Omar El Dansuri sat at the expansive mahogany desk that had become his following his brother's demise. Their father, King Rafael, had unofficially stepped down a few weeks ago owing to failing health, and Majid was to have succeeded him. The stipulation of marriage before ascension to the throne had led to the speedy conclusion of the treaty between Sudar and Bagumi, as well as the marriage between Majid and India barely a month after their first meeting.

His brother should have been the one sitting at this desk right now, carrying the weight of a troubled nation on his shoulders. Without preamble, fate had thrust this responsibility on him; a position he wouldn't have been eligible for just half a century ago when ascension to the throne had required full Sudari bloodlines. His mother had been the daughter of a paramount chief from Northern Ghana, but her royal lineage didn't matter to the purists, nor did the fact that he'd never met her. His mother had died in childbirth, and he'd been raised by Queen Azmera, Majid's biological mother, as her own.

The same purists now stood against many of his reforms aimed at turning the kingdom's economy around—in particular, his campaign for Sudar to join the

African Union and allow foreign diplomatic missions in. There were also many who agreed with his thinking, but the traditionalists believed opening up Sudar would affect the culture and traditions negatively.

A big proponent of this theory was his own uncle Sheikh Latif, Emir of the semi-autonomous state of Umm Jafar, who was next in line until Omar produced an heir. Although Uncle Latif had shown unwavering support for King Rafael, and even for Majid, he didn't misuse any opportunity to comment about what he would do differently if he were king.

Omar, on the other hand, had never desired the throne of Sudar with all its encumbrances, never coveted anything due his brother as the heir.

Until he'd set eyes on India Saene.

He remembered it clearly—walking into this very room. They'd been sitting on the comfortable sofas where the king received his guests; his father and brother on one, and King Ibrahim Saene of Bagumi and his daughter, India, on the other.

The moment he'd entered, his gaze had collided with hers, and for five whole seconds, everything in him had stilled. He'd only been released from her ensnaring eyes when his father had spoken, introducing her as Majid's fiancée. A sharp jolt had rocked his chest, a stab of jealousy, for the first time, for something belonging to his brother.

He'd torn his eyes away, making a mental note to stay as far away from her as possible, because even with the knowledge of her being his future sister-in-law, he'd still been too aware of her almond-shaped eyes, her succulent-looking lips, and the rise and fall of her breasts.

He wished he could have dismissed it as a passing fancy, or a result of a self-imposed celibacy, but three months without action didn't quite qualify as abstinence. He'd gone longer without sex and hadn't reacted in such a primal way to the first female he'd set eyes on.

His awareness of her had grown when she'd spoken about protecting children and creating equal opportunities for women in the sub-region, especially where old mind-sets still existed. She'd been eloquent, her voice echoing with intelligence and passion. For one unguarded moment, his mind had led him on an excursion of forbidden thoughts, and he'd wondered if she exhibited similar passion in other areas.

Now, she was his.

Her look of disbelief when he'd given her the news of their marriage had haunted him all afternoon. Though she hadn't said it, he sensed she meant to fight against their union. He had a feeling, too, that he knew why. She'd been willing to sacrifice her happiness to the marriage alliance when she'd been somewhat a part of the process.

This time, actions had been taken without her knowledge, and while their two fathers were within their rights for going ahead with the inheritance rights, his crash course on India Saene told him she wouldn't see it that way. She would most certainly fight him on this the moment she could get out of the hospital bed.

Normally, his default position to the marriage would have been resistance; a self-professed non-conformist, he'd always gotten a kick from doing the unexpected—a characteristic that had earned him the moniker Royal Pain, but even that had been like a badge of honour to his young self.

The trouble-making Omar had disappeared the day Majid died, fundamentally altering his priorities and killing his inert need for owning the shock factor.

Even if this weren't the case, he couldn't pretend he didn't desire India. Now that she was his, he didn't plan on letting her go. He just needed to figure out how to win her heart before it was too late.

Taking a deep breath, he returned his attention to the dossier in front of him and his head of security, sitting across from him, a man in his forties who looked ten years younger and could still take down a twenty-year-old without batting an eyelid.

"Are you sure about this, Khaya?" he asked. "It wasn't an accident?"

"Yes, Sire, I'm sure," General Khaya said. "The collision appears to be an accident. Wrong place, wrong time. However, the car's tires were definitely tampered with to orchestrate the blowout."

Omar swore as anger ballooned inside him, along with a side order of guilt. He shouldn't have put stock in the semblance of peace that had reigned for the past eight months since neutralising the royal family's biggest opposition. Unlike Majid whose mistrust of people had become second nature, Omar still believed in the general good of people.

During his time in the army, he'd seen the best and worst of humanity. Instead of becoming disillusioned like some of his colleagues, he'd instead chosen the path of hope.

After his tour of duty, he'd spent years abroad, managing the kingdom's global business interests and amassing considerable wealth for The Crown. During this time, he'd learned the value of diplomacy. Human beings may not be inherently good, but most would choose to be good with enough incentive. Or so he'd thought.

The result? The enemies of the throne had succeeded in laying their hands on the heir of Sudar. He should have been more vigilant, knowing his brother had been busy finalising the details of the alliance as well as the wedding. He'd see to it all responsible were brought to justice if it was the last thing he did.

"What do we know about the people behind it?" he asked, his deathly calm voice belying the rage roiling in his chest.

"Not a lot, Sire," came the less than satisfactory response. "When we captured the Nassiru gang a year ago, we had reason to believe the threat had been neutralised. We've been monitoring their activities."

"Find every last one of their allies," Omar said. "After they taste my brand of justice, they'll desire death, but I won't be so merciful."

"Your Royal Highness, this wasn't the Nassiru gang. Whatever survived our raid won't have the resources to pull off something like this. It was too seamless."

Omar sensed hesitation in Khaya's answer.

"What are you not telling me?"

"Sire, I believe whoever did this had help."

"What about the driver of the other vehicle?"

"Still in a coma, and it doesn't look good. He wasn't wearing a seatbelt, so we have to assume it was unrelated, or he intended to commit suicide. We don't know whether his motivation was of a personal or religious nature."

He swore. His father had spent a great deal of resources to create opportunities for the youth of Sudar precisely to keep them from wandering into the hands of people with extremist agendas. Was this evidence of failure? Or just an outlier who'd fallen through the cracks?

"We ran his prints through our database, but it yielded no results. None of our allies have been able to identify him."

"Any other suspects?"

"No, Sire."

"Find me one," Omar barked. "Until you do, I'll need daily updates on your investigation."

"Yes, Sire."

"I also want a list of everyone who had access to the car that day."

"Of course, Sire."

"If there's nothing else, you may go. Please inform Waheed I'll be driving myself to the hospital today."

"Sire?" Khaya said, drawing Omar's attention. "May I ask what arrangements are in place for after Her Royal Highness is discharged from the hospital?"

"She comes home." He raised his brows. "What is it, Khaya?"

"The would-be queen may want to go home to Bagumi and seek the support of her family."

Omar shook his head. "I can't guarantee her safety if I let her leave my protection, so unless I'm able to travel with her, she's going to stay here in Sudar."

Khaya nodded, seemingly satisfied with the response. "A wise decision, Sire."

With that, the head of security bowed and exited the room.

Alone again, Omar pondered Khaya's question, wondering if he should have probed further. When it came to India, it seemed his mind didn't function as well as it usually did, while other parts of his anatomy operated on overdrive.

He checked the time on his phone. *Five o'clock.* Time to wrap up at the office and head over to visit her at the hospital.

CHAPTER TWO

Three days later, India was discharged. Five o'clock found her dressed and ready to leave, even though Omar had told her she'd be picked up at six. Walking over to the window, she gazed two stories down. From where she stood, in the VVIP wing of the hospital, she only had a view of a portion of the car park.

A noise at the door made her turn. She smiled as she noticed the three bouquets of flowers her personal assistant carried.

"More flowers from well-wishers, My Lady," Salma said.

She'd been receiving get-well messages and flowers every day since she'd regained consciousness. Actually, she'd been told they'd started pouring in since Day One.

Imminent tears burned and brimmed at her eyes. Normally not given to emotions, she blinked and cleared her throat. "How can they show me so much love when I'm the reason Prince Majid is dead?"

"It was an act of God, Princess India," Salma said. "No one could have predicted it."

Her mind drifted to the accident—or what she remembered of it. The conversation, the loud bang, the car swerving, Majid's shout, the other car's headlights. It had all happened so fast, but before then, nothing had seemed amiss.

She shook off the thoughts, receiving the flowers from Salma. The fresh scent brought on another smile.

"The people may have lost their prince," Salma said. "But with your marriage to His Royal Highness, they have gained a princess."

She regarded the other woman for a moment. Perhaps having a Sudari PA wasn't such a bad idea. It would help her to get to know the people and culture faster. She'd been unhappy to let her regular assistant go, but Amal had a husband who worked for her father and three children. It wouldn't have been fair to expect her to leave her loved ones and move to Sudar with her.

"The people of Sudar must have impossibly big hearts."

"Perhaps they are just tired of bad news," Salma replied. "Now that you're going home, there's some good news to look forward to. People are already talking about the coronation."

"Coronation?" She frowned. "Omar hasn't been crowned? What is he waiting for?"

Her PA hesitated.

"I think you should ask him." Before India had a chance to probe, Salma asked, "Would you be taking the flowers home?"

India shook her head, not missing the quick change in subject. "I'm sure there are other patients who could use some cheering up."

A smile of approval touched Salma's lips. "I'll see to it."

"Before you go, can I ask you a question?"

"Of course, My Lady."

"Who packed my bags?"

"His Royal Highness saw to it himself."

"I see."

Movement outside the glass doors caught her attention, and she stilled.

Omar.

Flanked by two bodyguards. One an older gentleman—in his forties, she guessed—and a younger one who looked to be in his thirties. Her gaze caught Omar's, and her body's response was immediate—heart pounding, breath snagging, body tingling with awareness. His grey caftan had intricate embroidery on the neckline and cuffs. She frowned. Hadn't he been wearing a suit this morning? Or was that yesterday?

He'd been visiting morning and evening every day, and even without wanting to, she'd found herself looking forward to his visits. He hadn't kissed her again, much to her relief, but his eyes always emitted heat and intent, which took her mind there, anyway, filling her with anticipation. It was worse than being kissed.

Expectation signified emotion; but that had no place in the alliance. She'd prepared for duty with Majid, not desire. Yet, each time Omar came near her, each time he looked into her eyes, she struggled to maintain her practical head on her shoulders.

He entered the room, but the bodyguards stayed outside.

"Ready to go?"

Her gaze dropped to his lips—generous, well-defined lips that looked chiselled; yet, she remembered their softness when he'd pressed them against her temple the other day. She shook her head. She may have gotten a clean bill of health, but the accident must have screwed with her mind, making her more vulnerable to his special brand of allure.

"Salma tells me you haven't had your coronation," she said, more to give her mind something else to focus on.

"No. I haven't been crowned."

"Why not?"

He paused, but before he could answer, Salma cleared her throat. "I'll take the flowers to the head nurse now, My Lady."

India diverted her attention to Salma and couldn't help thinking the woman was running. "Very well, Salma."

When her PA had left, she took in a breath and returned her gaze to Omar who stood only a couple of feet away. Funny, his brother had been taller, but she'd never had the sensation of being drowned by him. Next to Omar, however, she felt like a delicate little flower. He seemed to tower over her, large and immovable.

"Isn't the stipulation for your coronation that you marry first? Which, according to you, we are."

"I assure you, India, we're married," he said. "However, in Sudari tradition, marriage is only confirmed through consummation."

Her eyes widened, and she nearly choked on her own saliva. It took every ounce of effort to keep her mouth from gaping. "Wh—what?"

She'd read about cultures where newlywed couples had to make love in the presence of family elders to confirm they'd slept together. She'd never imagined such a thing would still be practiced in the twenty-first century.

Clearly, she should have done a more thorough investigation about Sudar before agreeing to marry into their royal family.

Ha! As if she'd had a choice.

"Your family expects to witness your first night with your bride?"

With a casual wave of his hand, he replied. "Of course not. That would just be primitive."

He spoke with a mild French-ness to his 'r'. It was sexy as hell. Try as she might, she couldn't squelch the images it pushed into her mind; images of being slowly undressed by Omar, of his hands and lips running lightly over her skin, of succumbing to his virility, allowing him to do the things his one kiss had put in her head.

The flames burning her face cascaded over the rest of her body. She fought to calm her erratic heartbeat. "How would they know we've consummated?"

"Nothing you'll be uncomfortable with," he replied. "It would suffice that you and I spend the night in the same bedroom."

"Even if we don't, erm…consummate?"

Had someone switched off the AC?

A beat passed.

His right brow hooked up. "Are you against…consummation?"

Was that a smile? Did he think this was funny? Time to shake off the deer in headlights sensation and take charge of this situation.

She swallowed. "Of course not."

"I take it to mean you're not a virgin. Good," he said.

She raised her brows.

"When you've had me, I want you to know the difference." His eyes gleamed. "Tell me, Princess India, have you had an orgasm before?"

Her eyes widened, but she stopped short of gasping at his audacity. "I don't see how that's relevant to you."

"I'm your husband. That makes your pleasure of paramount importance to me."

"Since I didn't agree to or participate in a wedding with you, I'd say you're getting way ahead of yourself, Omar."

He leaned forward, and she began to tingle all over. Though he hadn't touched her, she could feel his heat radiating into her. She stopped breathing for a couple of seconds. Did he mean to kiss her? Exert some dominance over her? Why didn't the idea fill her with righteous indignation?

"Aren't you even a little curious about the notes I can make you sing with just my tongue?"

A smile of pure male satisfaction came to his lips at her sharp intake of breath. God, she was in trouble.

Determined to have the last laugh, however, she squared her shoulders. "Not in the least."

"Given the way the soft skin at the base of your lovely neck is pumping, *ya jameel*, I call bull." He pulled back, abandoning the seductive smile. "Besides, need I remind you why your country needs this alliance?"

Her lips parted, ready to dish out a response, but her brain didn't oblige. He was right. Bagumi couldn't back out of this alliance. A recent economic downturn in Bagumi had led to her father accepting a substantial financial investment from Sudar as part of her bride wealth. Going back on this alliance meant losing that aid, which would mean going to an international body and committing to a sovereign debt that would be detrimental in the long run.

"I'm not just going to take your word that we're married."

"By all means." He fished out a cell phone from his pocket. "You're welcome to call your father."

His confidence spoke volumes, and even as she took the device, she had a feeling she wasn't going to like the conversation she with her father.

She dialled her father's direct line, and he picked almost instantly. She greeted him in Bagumese.

"India." He had a smile in his voice, which she took as a good sign. "I'm sorry I couldn't be there for your release from hospital, but the doctor advises you rest. Having all of us there might be counterproductive."

She smiled, nodding. Given the chance, the whole battalion of her family would be here, offering support. "That's okay, Baba. I'm sure the doctor will clear me to travel back home soon."

"No, my daughter. We'll visit when you're feeling stronger. Your home is now in Sudar."

"So it's true? I'm married to Omar?" Silence greeted her question. "You allowed this?"

Her father's sigh carried over.

"India, you're the most level-headed among my daughters, so I won't sugar-coat it. After Amira broke her engagement to Prince Duak, the only way to maintain peace was to relinquish our rights to the waters bordering Bagumi and Ashani. It has come at a great cost to our kingdom."

And I'm the sacrificial lamb.

A stretch of silence followed before her father continued. "We need the alliance with Sudar."

She hated to hear the despondency in her father's voice, but she loved him and her kingdom. She wouldn't let either of them down without trying.

"Okay, Baba. I'll stay in Sudar for now."

After a little more conversation, she ended the call. She'd expected a self-satisfied smile from Omar when she returned the phone, but he appeared sombre; a tad sympathetic, even. Taking in a deep breath, she headed out after him, determined to keep her word to her father. Until she could find a way of getting out of it.

***

Omar wasn't taking chances. Since the accident and his subsequent ascension to would-be king, he travelled with full security detail. He'd decided on this even before the confirmation of foul play, which made it even more important for him to take extra precautions. He could have had the road closed, but that would have been a dead give-away.

This evening, top among his priorities was to assure India of her safety while keeping a low profile. They left the building through a private exit and travelled in an unmarked vehicle between two security vehicles and a third one a couple of cars behind.

With that aspect of the journey taken care of, he had nothing left to do but enjoy the one-hour ride to his private residence while feasting his eyes on India. She stared ahead, appearing calm, but her hands, balled into fists by her sides, told him otherwise. What must she be thinking and feeling?

He reached out and took her hand. She responded with a sharp inhalation before glancing in his direction, giving him a slight lift of her lips in a cursory smile most likely meant to distract him from her nervousness.

"It will get better," he said, guessing she might be thinking about the last time she'd been in a car. It may also have been for his own comfort as he imagined what his brother must have been thinking when the accident happened.

Was it too soon to ask her to relive it? She'd have to do it at some point. Anything she remembered could be useful for the investigation, but he also needed to know, perhaps as a means of getting closure.

There would be time. He and India had the next few days to themselves during which he would get her to open up in more ways than one. He sat back. He was getting ahead of himself. His focus should be firmly on getting Majid's killers and keeping the rest of the family safe.

"What about you?" she said. "How are you coping?"

He released a breath. "You're the first person to ask."

Her brows hooked up. "Really?"

He nodded. "I'm expected to take the mantle as king, to be strong and lead the kingdom, and to show no weakness."

"You lost a brother."

"You lost a husband."

"I only met your brother five times before we married. We barely knew each other, but you two grew up together," she responded.

True enough, but for several years in the past, he and Majid had barely spoken. The thought filled him with regret for running instead of facing up to his brother for something he believed in, memories he didn't wish to recall.

"Why are you riding with me?" she said out of the blue. "I thought it was against protocol."

"The rule only applies to public and high-risk events when it's most important to safeguard the royal family." To reassure her, he added, "I've taken precautions to ensure this journey is as discreet as possible."

With a heavy exhalation, she returned to staring ahead. He noted, though, that her hands were no longer balled into fists.

The rest of the journey continued in silence.

He didn't take her to his official residence at the palace but to a private place he kept under a pseudonym—a hideout known to a select few.

When they arrived, he exited the car, just as General Khaya—who, as an added precaution, had taken the lead to check for any security breaches—approached.

"Welcome, Sire," Khaya said.

"Good evening, Khaya. Anything to report?"

"All clear."

"And on the investigation?"

The head of security seemed to hesitate. "There is something to report."

Omar sucked in a breath. Any new information could get them closer to whoever committed the heinous crime against his family and the kingdom.

"Meet me in my office. I'll join you after we've settled in."

***

India remained in the car until Omar returned. He opened the door, and she stepped out. The main house was well-lit. On the outside, a solitary light on top of the door illuminated their path. Beyond that, there appeared to be trees, but in the darkness, she couldn't determine how dense.

"Where are we?"

"My hideaway home," he answered. "The doctor said you need rest, so I didn't want to take you to the palace yet. We'll do that in a week or so. Come with me."

Relief washed over her. She hadn't considered it before, but she realised in retrospect that she wasn't ready to face the rest of his family, or the kingdom, for that matter. She didn't know what she'd say to King Rafael or Queen Azmera.

She stepped forward, then stopped as a dizzy sensation swept over her and everything began to spin. Unable to regain her balance, she reached for the hand he proffered. She missed, and a gasp left her lips.

Thankfully, Omar was faster. His arms closed around her waist. The contact was electric, zapping away any remnants of dizziness.

Instead of setting her upright, he inclined her further, sliding his right arm down to the back of her knees and lifting her off the ground.

"I'm fine. You can put me down now."

It pleased her to note how steady her voice sounded. At least, he wasn't privy to the upheaval in her system resulting from his touch.

"It's customary for a husband to carry his bride over the threshold."

She sucked in a breath, determined to quash the warmth drizzling down to her centre. Their union might be legitimate, but it remained a marriage of alliance. They didn't need to indulge in romanticisms.

She started to push against his chest. Muscles rippled under her palms, sending waves of excitement through her. She snatched her hands away, darting a glance at him. Heat blazed her face and everywhere her body touched his. It was ridiculous that she reacted to every contact with him. He, on the other hand, appeared unaffected, as if carrying a woman against his solid chest was something he did often.

Best to let him win the battle. After all, once they entered the house, he'd have to set her down. He carried her up three steps, and the massive double doors swung open.

The old gentleman, clearly the butler, stepped aside with a bow. "Welcome home, Sire."

"Thank you, Karim," Omar said while India managed a small smile and a nod.

When they entered, he didn't put her down as she'd hoped but continued through a foyer and up a flight of stairs.

"Where are you taking me?"

"To our bedroom," he said as if it were the most natural thing in the world.

"Bedroom?" she blurted out. "*Our* bedroom?"

She'd thought he'd been joking about sharing the same room. Apparently not.

He looked at her, brows raised, a glint of amusement in his eyes. "I'm not going to jump your bones, if that's what you're thinking."

Desire jolted through her, pooling in a moist sensation at the apex of her thighs. She clamped her thighs together in a firm decision to overlook her heightened awareness of him. What was it about Omar that had her on edge and permanently thinking about sex? She disregarded her thudding heart and tried to ignore the tips of his fingers skirting the base of her breast.

She didn't breathe until they entered the bedroom and he eased her into a seated position on her bed. He crouched in front of her, taking her left foot in his hands. He slipped off her wedge heels, then gently massaged her sole for a few seconds. Her muscles relaxed while her breath hiked. He repeated the action with her other foot.

"Lie down and get some rest," he said after releasing her. "I have to attend to an urgent matter."

By this time, she was fairly certain any verbal protests would sound breathy or squeaky and reveal to him exactly how much he'd affected her. Silently, she complied, welcoming the comfort of the soft sheets with a sigh.

***

Five minutes later, Omar entered his office where General Khaya waited for him. His gaze zoomed in on the folder in the other man's possession.

"What do you have for me, General?"

"We have a lead, Sire."

"What kind of lead?"

He knew better than to celebrate prematurely, but he couldn't help entertaining a spark of hope. He could avenge his brother, find the people behind the plot to overthrow the monarchy, ensure the safety of his family, and focus on moving the country forward.

"A suspect, Sire."

"Why isn't this person on his knees before me begging for mercy?"

Khaya shifted. In all the years he'd known the man, Omar hadn't seen him show uncertainty about anything. His reluctance to the deliver the news spoke volumes.

"Who is it? A known enemy?" *No.* That would be expected. "An ally turned hostile?"

"It's the princess, Sire."

"What princess?"

"The princess consort."

Omar reared back. "India? You think she's behind the accident? In case you missed it, she was also in the car."

"They were to have travelled separately as per Sudari rules, but Majid broke protocol and insisted they rode together since they had just married."

"Please tell me you have more than that."

"We have transcripts of a phone conversation." He offered the file in his hand.

Omar didn't take it. "What does it say?"

General Khaya opened the file and read. "The day before the wedding, Her Royal Highness received a message saying 'on stand-by for tomorrow,' and she replied with a thumbs-up. The day of the wedding, after the ceremony, a few minutes before they embarked on the journey, she received another message, 'are we a go?' She responded, 'abort. M Not alone'."

"Em?"

"The letter, Sire. Most likely a typo or alternative to I'm."

"It could mean anything."

"Yes, Sire," General Khaya replied. "Except she had deleted the messages. We used a third-party app to retrieve them."

That sounded bad, he supposed. He still had his doubts.

"Sire, there's one more thing. We also know Her Royal Highness explicitly inquired about whether the alliance would hold if either of them passed on prematurely."

That stopped Omar cold, forcing him to entertain the possibility of India being a viable suspect. He couldn't continue to reject the notion no matter how much he wanted to.

"Do we know who she was communicating with?"

The general shook his head. "A private number. Untraceable."

"What other angles are we looking at?"

"This is the only lead we have now, Sire," Khaya said. "While we work to eliminate her as a suspect, we need to ensure she stays in Sudar."

"Done," Omar said. "General, I don't need to remind you about the treaty we've just signed with her country. I have no problem making her face the full rigours of our laws, but before I accuse Bagumi's princess of assassination, I need the smoking gun."

"Working on it, Your Royal Highness."

CHAPTER THREE

India woke up the next morning, filled with a lightness of being she hadn't felt in weeks. She sucked in a deep breath, let it fill her lungs. She held it for a few seconds before releasing it. She'd missed waking up in a comfortable bed surrounded by soft sheets rather than stiff cotton sheets, stark white walls, and the constant beeping of medical machines.

Home sweet home. Her eyes fluttered open, and the unfamiliar sight of an elegant bedroom brought on a sudden wave of consciousness.

She was miles from home. Married to Prince Omar El Dansuri. *Inherited,* she corrected, still trying to wrap her mind around it. She'd been prepared for battle, but her chat with her father yesterday had stolen the fight out of her. Bagumi couldn't afford to return the bride wealth Sudar had paid under the guise of an investment to enable her country to maintain certain economic markers after having to give up their border rights to the neighbouring kingdom of Ashani. Failure to do so could mean losing their bid for membership in the African Union.

She didn't want to recall the conversation, which had confirmed Omar's claim. The cherry on top the cake had been the reminder that her marriage was about the union between Bagumi and Sudar and nothing to do with her desires or happiness.

She shook her head. She knew wife inheritance still existed in certain remote parts of the continent. She hadn't expected it in Sudar, so close to home.

She cast a look around the expansive room. *Our bedroom.* Omar's voice echoed in her head. She sat up so fast, she feared her head would spin. Thankfully, being seated helped. She shot a glance to the other side of the bed, noted the dip in the pillow. Definitely slept-in.

A shiver ran up her spine at the knowledge that she'd slept in the same bed as Omar. He'd kept his promise of not jumping her. *A man of his word.* She didn't know much about him but suspected her assessment was correct. A good thing. Because the truth was that Omar scared her. His masculinity overwhelmed her senses. It wasn't just about his looks. She'd grown up with four brothers who took the cake in the looks department. Her brothers also came with varying degrees of the Alpha gene, so it couldn't be that, either.

Something about Omar's obsidian eyes made her feel exposed every time he looked into hers. God knew she wasn't the most sexually experienced person on the planet, but he made her think about hot kisses and naked bodies and tangled sheets.

She cast a glance around the large bedroom, sighed when she spotted her handbag in a luxe dresser nested by a door to what she assumed to be an en-suite bathroom. She threw off the sheets and got out of the king-sized bed. Her bare feet sank into the lush carpet as she walked over to her bag.

As expected, she found her phone on the dresser next to the bag. Beside it lay a piece of paper bearing her name in cursive writing. She took the note and unfolded it.

Breakfast will be ready at seven.

She noted how he wrote the time in words rather than numerals like every normal person. He wasn't any ordinary person, she reminded herself. He was the next king of Sudar; the man who would ensure free trade lines between Bagumi and Northern Africa, which would boost the economies of both kingdoms.

Putting Omar and the alliance out of her mind, she pressed the home button on her phone. *Six forty-five.* That gave her enough time to take a quick shower and get dressed.

Fifteen minutes later, she stepped out of the bedroom chamber to the outer room of the suite. As if on cue, a knock sounded at the door.

"Enter," she said, wondering why Omar would knock.

The door swung open, and the butler entered. Salim? Karim?

"Good morning, My Lady," he said with a bow. "My name is Karim. I am tasked with showing you to the dining room."

"Thank you, Karim."

When Omar had called it his hideaway home, she'd expected a comfortable but modest house lacking any form of opulence. As she followed the butler, however, she noted the white and gold walls displaying various works of art and the elegant furniture. In an open foyer leading out to five different areas, the intricate *trompe-l'œil* painting on the ceiling gave the impression of a dome. She wanted to pause and admire the artistry of it, but she was already late for breakfast.

Karim led her through the archway entry to the dining room, and India stopped short as her gaze settled on her breakfast companion. Not Omar. A woman. Her eyes zoomed in on the ring-bearing finger. For several seconds, she stood frozen as, with horror, she realised she hadn't considered this possibility at all. She wasn't Omar's only wife.

She shouldn't be surprised. Polygyny was widely practiced in many parts of the continent. Even in her family. Her father, King Ibrahim, had two wives, and out of her six siblings, only two, Zik and Isha, were from the same mother. Yet, there wasn't much rivalry between her father's wives or between her and her siblings. Despite this love she'd grown up with, she'd always expected to be the only love of her future husband. A pipedream, obviously, for a woman who didn't have the liberty to choose who she'd marry.

The lady at the dining table lifted her eyes and smiled. "I was wondering when you'd arrive. I'm Janae."

"Pleased to meet you, Janae." India forced a smile. She should be grateful. Having Janae around would help insulate her from Omar's magnetism. So why did her chest suddenly feel like someone had stuck a jagged-edged knife in and pulled? "I didn't realise the wives ate alone."

"Wife?" Janae raised her brows and laughed. "He should be so lucky. I'm not Omar's wife."

"Oh?"

In reflex, her gaze darted to Janae's hand, and she noted belatedly that the ring was on her right hand. She tried to ignore the relief sweeping through her while admonishing herself in no uncertain terms. It didn't matter that this beautiful woman wasn't a rival for Omar's affections.

"I'm his aunt. Although I'm only older by three years. A surprise baby, if you like," she explained. "My nephew has royal matters to handle this morning and thought you'd need company, so here I am."

Something twisted in her chest, which she refused to think about and rather tried to focus on the conversation.

"Join me," Janae said. "You must be hungry."

She nodded and took a seat at the table next to Janae. Now that she knew who the woman was, she found herself appraising her with new eyes.

"You don't look your age. You certainly don't appear to be older than Omar."

"That's because he's always brooding. I call him an old soul. Thirty going on fifty."

India couldn't help smiling as Omar's intense gazes came to mind.

"He's always acted older than his years," Janae continued with a fondness in her voice. "Always wanted to do things before he was old enough. Thank you for the compliment, though. Now I know why the nation is in love with you."

"I don't know about that. Maybe they are just tired of bad news," India replied, remembering her conversation with Salma.

A moment of silence ensued while she helped herself to some freshly baked bread buns and fruit salad. Karim came to pour some herbal tea into her cup. After they were alone again, Janae looked at India's plate.

"Do you always eat like a bird?"

India laughed. "I'm not a huge breakfast person. Usually, I get by with a cup of tea or coffee, two slices of wheat bread, and whatever fruit is in season."

"A healthy eater."

"Just the plight of a woman who doesn't like exercising, much to my brother Zareb's dismay," she confessed.

"That's the former Olympian, right?"

She nodded. "I have a weakness for chocolate, though."

Janae closed her eyes briefly and moaned. "A woman after my very heart. When you finally move into the palace, I'll introduce you the best double chocolate cake you've ever eaten."

"You bake?"

"Oh, no. Not me. The palace chef, Pierre. He's Ivorian, trained in his country as well as Paris."

They continued to chat while eating. By the time the meal ended, India felt like she'd known Janae for years. In a sense, Omar's young, vivacious aunt reminded her of her own sister, Isha.

"How are you holding up?" Janae asked when they had finished eating.

India inhaled deeply, releasing it slowly, buying time. "To be honest, I'm not sure. A part of me feels numb with the shock of knowing I could have been dead. The other part of me wonders why I lived and Majid didn't."

"Survivor's guilt." Janae reached out and gave her hand a gentle squeeze. "Don't blame yourself. The universe has plans we don't always understand. Majid would have hated himself if it had been the other way around."

Nothing appropriate came to mind for a response, so she just nodded.

"Shall we move to the drawing room?" Janae asked. "I have an album to show you. Must-see places for when you're ready to step out."

Just as they stood, Omar walked in. Her breath caught at the sight of him. Dressed in jeans and a casual, loose-fitting dashiki which nonetheless draped over his broad shoulders like a lover, he oozed sex appeal in droves. His gaze caught on hers, held for a couple seconds before shifting to his aunt.

"There's been a change of plans," he announced. "I'll be staying home with India today, so I'm relieving you of your duties. The driver will take you back to the palace."

"Something wrong?" Janae asked.

"I took your advice about spending time with my new bride."

India swallowed, her heart racing. Alone with Omar? She wanted to protest, but ripples of excitement stole into her and clogged her throat.

"Well, who am I to stand in the way of a budding love?"

India frowned. *Love?* What was the other woman smoking?

Janae stretched up and kissed Omar's cheek, then turned, her back to him, and winked at India. With that, she breezed out of the room.

India returned her attention to Omar. His unsmiling face returned her stare without giving her the benefit of reading his expression.

"We need to talk, but not here." He turned and started walking. "Come with me."

Seeing no other choice, she followed, practically jogging to keep up with his strides. Instinct told her something was wrong, in spite of what he'd told Janae.

She dogged his steps through a door leading to a magnificent, wood-panelled office, rich and elegant and as masculine as its owner. He whipped round suddenly. She gasped, stopping short of crashing into his solid chest. Luckily, the two-second pause to admire the office had bought her just enough time and space to stop.

They stood inches apart, and for several seconds, his heated gaze bore into hers before dropping to her lips. Her heart rate spiked as the heat of anticipation and awareness deluged her body.

He retreated a few steps, flicked his right hand. "Sit down."

She turned and noticed a leather sofa a few steps to her left. Still disoriented from her near-collision with him, she found herself doing as he commanded. He distanced himself, reaching his massive desk in a few unhurried steps and leaning against it.

"Tell me about the accident."

Her heart, which had almost relented to its normal rate, tripped over a beat and resumed an erratic tempo.

She shook her head. "You said you wouldn't push me until I was ready. I'm not."

"I'm afraid the situation has changed," he replied. "I can no longer keep my word."

"Why not? What changed between last night and this morning?"

"We have a new lead in the investigation."

"A lead? You think it wasn't an accident?"

"I don't think," he said. "I know."

She sat back trying to assimilate the information. She'd heard news about unrest in parts of the country, with some even calling for the abolition of the monarchy. Did people want this so badly that they'd be prepared to see it done at any cost? As a public figure and a member of a royal family, she was used to bodyguards especially during public events, but she'd simply learnt to ignore them, mentally making them part of the background. A necessary evil to keep her father happy.

She'd never experienced a blatant attempt on her life, and the idea that someone had targeted Omar's brother put a sick feeling in her stomach. If any detail she could remember would help, she needed to set aside her own discomfort.

"What do you need to know?"

"Anything you can remember."

She allowed her mind to drift back to that day, remembering the proud look on her father's face as he'd kissed her forehead before she'd embarked on the private plane with Majid, the happy Sudari crowd that had met them at the airport. Every security arrangement had appeared normal. Taking in a deep breath, she narrated the experience, hoping something new would occur to her, anything the investigators would find useful in bringing the culprit to justice.

A few seconds elapsed after she'd ended her narration. What was he thinking? She tried assessing Omar's disposition. This couldn't be easy for him. However, he'd schooled his expression, hiding whatever was going on within him. A part of her wanted to reach out and comfort him, but she restrained herself.

His loss didn't change the fact that he'd married her, not only without her consent, but he'd done it while she lay unconscious in a hospital bed. If that didn't warn her to keep her distance, she didn't know what would. Omar was not a good person. She needed to keep that in mind.

He picked up a file from the desk and marched to her side, tossing it on the empty space beside her.

"Can you tell me the meaning of these messages?"

She frowned at him, then at the folder before picking it up and flipping it open. Her eyes widened as she read the messages that looked awfully familiar.

"What is this?" she asked.

"You tell me. They're from your mobile phone."

A sickening feeling slithered down her spine. The implication of his words and icy stare hit her like a splash of cold water.

"Are you accusing me of something?"

"If the cap fits."

Disbelief rocked her. She'd almost died, and he thought she had something to do with it? Anger flared.

"You invaded my privacy!"

"There's no privacy for people who commit treason."

She gasped. "T—treason?"

"That's normally what we call the offense of acting to overthrow, harm, or kill our sovereign," he said, his voice composed, as if he'd had time to gather his thoughts and plan his actions. "Who are you working with, India?"

She began to tremble as something occurred to her anew. Aside from the butler, she'd seen no servant since arriving yesterday. He'd sent Janae away, and for all she knew, the butler, too, had been given a day off, meaning they were alone. She was at Omar's mercy!

"You lied," she said. "You didn't bring me here to recuperate. This is a detention."

"For the record, I don't lie. I brought you here to get better, but I came to meet this new piece of information, so we're staying here until you either confess or my people get the evidence I need."

"I can't confess to something I didn't do."

"Then we wait for the evidence."

"This is ridiculous. My father will hear of this." She picked up her phone.

"You're wasting your time," he said. "I've activated a signal blocker. You can't reach anyone or vice versa."

She swallowed. "Are you saying I'm a prisoner?"

"Until further notice." He gave her a cold stare that put ice in her veins. "The only reason I'm giving you this privilege of privacy is because you also happen to be my wife and the would-be queen of Sudar."

"You can't cut me off from my family and my work."

Panic began to set in. She should probably not be thinking about work, but what she did ensured thousands of children across the continent had at least one decent meal a day and a place to sleep at night. As patron of the Queen Nayanka Foundation, named after her grandmother, she had to oversee the organisation of the annual Children's Foundation end-of-year fundraising gala. Granted, the end of the year was more than ten months away, but for an international function that attracted thousands of dignitaries from around the world, ten months was barely enough time.

Thankfully, even though she took a hands-on approach when it came to some of the foundation's activities, she had a team back in Bagumi working with the foundation's satellite offices in Accra and Lagos. She could afford a few days off without fear of things falling through the cracks.

A humourless laugh broke out of him, putting an instant stop to her thoughts.

"You disappoint me, India. Has it not occurred to you? Thanks to you and your cronies, I'm the de-facto sovereign of Sudar. I can do pretty much what I want."

She stood, propelled by her shock and anger, then forced herself, on shaky legs, to take a step closer to him. "That much is very clear."

He sneered, closing the space between them. Her heart raced. He grabbed her jaw, forcing her to go on tiptoes. She clamped down on the impulse to flinch, determined not to show any signs of fear.

"This is how you treat your queen?" Her voice grated against strained vocal chords.

His grip eased a fraction, and he dropped his gaze to her lips. "No. I have far more pleasant plans for my queen."

Tears stung her eyes. She blinked them away. A man who had no qualms laying marital claims on a woman who had no ability to say no would have no problem taking what he might believe to be his husbandly rights.

She swallowed. "You can do whatever you please to my body, but I shall not yield to you."

Anger flashed in his eyes.

"Don't worry. If I ever make love to you, you'll have to beg for it."

She snorted. "I don't beg, and I don't intend to start with you."

"You say that now." With another sneer, he released her. "Lunch is at one."

With that, he turned and walked out of the room. She clutched her jaw, releasing a shaky breath. She had to find a way to contact her brother, Zareb. As head of Bagumian palace security, he would be able to get her out of here.

CHAPTER FOUR

Much to Omar's relief, India didn't show up for lunch. He wasn't prepared for another dose of her feisty personality, didn't need another occasion to resist those luscious, sassy lips of hers or to ignore the rise and fall of her chest as she hyperventilated in righteous anger.

He'd been harsh with her, but it had been a deliberate act to gauge her reaction to his accusation. The way a person responded under pressure said a lot about them, and he'd always had a sharp eye when it came to reading people. Thinking back at the indignation in her eyes, the trembling in her body when he'd held her, he was convinced she hadn't killed his brother.

Right now, though, his mind drifted back to the way his body had sprung alive when he'd caught her sweet scent, after her soft body had brushed against him.

Sleeping next to her last night had taken its toll, which meant he was already running low on resolve. Yes, there were two other rooms in the house, but neither of them had a bathroom fitted with a shower, and he was not a Jacuzzi man. Besides, when he'd checked in on her and found her asleep, he hadn't been able to walk away. He'd made sure to be up and out of there before she woke up, though. A good thing, apparently, since she thought him to be the kind of man—less than a man—who'd take pleasure from a woman without regard for her wishes.

Worse. She had every right to hold such an opinion of him. After all, he'd married her while she was still in a coma and whisked her off to this home in the middle of nowhere and told her she was his prisoner. He couldn't tell her why he'd had to marry her when he did. He'd been tempted after she'd hurled her accusation at him, but he'd known better than to act purely in satisfaction of his personal desires.

No. Another confrontation with her so soon after this morning would be detrimental to his sanity.

When she didn't show up for dinner, however, he got worried. No way was he letting her starve herself. If she wouldn't come for dinner, then he'd take food to her. Short of going to the room and dragging her out here, he saw no other choice. Since he'd already dismissed the cook, he had to go to the kitchen and spend five minutes searching for a suitable tray, one large enough to carry a variety of offerings.

Returning to the dining table, he dished out an assortment of meats, veggies, and sauces to go with the oven-roasted sweet potatoes and couscous. Then, he added a plate of fruits and baked desserts.

Satisfied with his selection, he carried the tray upstairs. He found her in the first chamber—not the bedroom, thankfully—sitting at the desk, scribbling on a notepad. In her left hand, she held an oatmeal bar, and in front of her sat a bottle of water.

She looked up and froze.

"An energy bar," he stated. "And here I was thinking you were starving."

She eyed the tray in his hand with interest, then made a show of taking a bite of the snack.

Without warning, laughter exploded out of him. He was happy to note the relaxation of her shoulders as he came to set the tray down in front of her.

When she raised the offensive excuse for a meal substitute to her mouth again, he caught her hand. She sucked in a breath, her gaze darting up. Electricity passed between them. He ignored the blood rushing to his groin as he took her hand and pulled the bar from her fingers.

"These things will kill you," he said.

"Unless you get to me first, right?"

A moment of silence followed.

"It's neither my intention nor my desire to kill you, but I'm not going to apologise for this morning," he said. "My brother has been assassinated. I want answers, and right now, you're the only one I know who has them."

"Although, if I don't tell you exactly what you want to hear, you'll just pin the crime on me."

He nearly laughed again. If only she knew how much he wanted her to be absolved of any suspicion, despite knowing the risks of letting a beautiful woman influence him. Thankfully, not from his own experience, but how many times had their father warned them about women? India already stood in the way of him taking his place on the throne, and he had only a couple of weeks to change her mind or risk losing the crown altogether.

He shook away the thought. He needed to focus on more urgent matters.

"I'd like to remove you from the suspect list. You can get the ball rolling by telling me who you were communicating with that day."

She may not have killed his brother, but their interaction in the morning had convinced him she was up to something. He needed to find out what, especially if it had implications for his people's safety or the throne of Sudar.

She looked straight in his eyes. "I can't tell you that, but I had nothing to do with your brother's death."

"Unfortunately, I can't take your word for it."

"The laws of Sudar." She gave a snort, pulling her hand from his grip. "Guilty until proven innocent."

He took in a breath, releasing it slowly. "If you're innocent, then this isolation may not be a bad idea. Whoever did this could target you."

"Why would they want to target me?"

"To make sure you don't remember any details that could lead to their arrest."

She seemed to consider this a moment, and worry briefly knitted in her brows. She stood and paced a few steps. Finally, she turned a fiery gaze on him.

"I've spent the day thinking, and I've come up with my own theory."

"Let's hear it."

At this point, he'd listen to any idea. The longer it took to catch the perpetrators, the higher the risk of never finding them.

"I asked myself who stands to gain from your brother's death. I've heard about militant groups in the south-west, but then, I remembered there's been a recent series of arrests made, foiling an attempted coup."

He raised a brow. Where was she going with this?

"If the militant group has been neutralised, then there's only one other person who stands to gain from this turn of events." She gave him a devilish smirk. "You, Omar."

"Me?" He blinked. "Your theory would have some basis if I desired to take the throne from my brother, but I've never wanted to be king."

"Unfortunately, I can't take your word for it."

He chuckled, recognising his own words cleverly thrown back at him. "Touché."

Her face remained unsmiling, her eyes expressing suspicion. He couldn't tell whether she was serious, but he had to give her credit for boldness. Most petite women would cower before his muscular, five-eleven stature, especially after the accusations he'd levelled against her earlier. Instead, she'd turned the tables on him.

"Here we are, two possible criminals stuck with each other for a week." He hoped his amusement didn't reflect in his voice lest she find offence in it. "I say we call a truce while we're here."

She didn't reply, but her defensive stance seemed to abate.

"Now, would you please eat something?"

Her gaze darted to the tray, but she shook her head. "You could have put something in it."

"To what end? Even if you were guilty of treason, I'd rather throw you in a Sudari jail where I'd control your personal hell than send you from this life and lose control over your punishment."

Maybe not the best response if he wanted to placate her. He released an exasperated sigh. "Fine, I'll be your royal taster."

He surveyed the options, his eyes settling on a slice of chocolate cake with milk chocolate frosting. *The way to a woman's heart is through chocolate.* The quote from Janae popped into his mind. Chocolate didn't do much for him, but his aunt swore by it, and since she happened to be one of the smartest women he knew, he picked a slice.

Walking up to her, he held it up and noted with satisfaction the slight pressing together of her lips as she swallowed. He took a bite, shaking his head and groaning for full effect. He took another bite, and when he sensed he'd baited her enough, he held the remaining piece a breath away from her lips.

"Your turn."

Indecision clouded her eyes.

"On the count of three, it disappears in my mouth. One...two..."

She parted her lips. He tried not to show his delight. She took a bite and made a sound, something between a whimper and a moan. *Sexy.* When he held the last piece before her, she accepted it without hesitation. Some of the frosting stuck to her lips like a pea-sized torture device meant to unravel him. He didn't know whether she'd noticed, so he decided to wipe it off for her. Just as his hand reached her lips, her tongue sneaked out, catching both the dollop of frosting and the tip of his thumb.

Blood rushed to his groin, ensuring the only thought in his head was the warmth of her tongue and how much he wanted to taste it. Before he could stop himself, his thumb touched her lips, gently tracing them.

He swallowed. "So soft."

She leaned in slightly, her lips parting. If he kissed her now, she'd be willing. A caution sounded in his head, but he ignored it. He'd promised not to make love to her, but he'd said nothing about kissing.

He leaned forward, a part of him hoping yet dreading she'd come to her senses and stop him from plunging into the deep end. Instead, she seemed to relax against him. His hand trailed the short distance from her lips to her chin, lifted her face.

He sipped her lips, gave her another tentative touch, a nibble. She acquiesced, granting him entry. At her invitation, he curved his other arm around her to palm the small of her back, then he crushed her against his body as the kiss took full possession of him, becoming more insistent.

Their tongues touched, and a little moan sounded from her, eliciting a groan from him. He tasted the chocolate cake. Another groan. Maybe he needed to reassess his opinion about chocolate, because right now, it felt like the best flavour in the world.

His hand moved up her back, caressing upward, lingering at her bra. His fingers toyed with the hooks. He could unclasp them through her dress. It would take seconds. Another moan from her. He should stop now.

No. He needed a little more, a little longer of this feeling, this intoxication. *Ya'Allah,* he needed to quit while he still had control of his faculties. When had he ever lacked restraint? Yet, even as his mind told him to stop while he was ahead, some unnamed part of him resisted. His lips and tongue acted of their own accord, favouring her taste over reason. The chocolate was gone, allowing him to savour the flavour that was uniquely her.

His hands explored her back, enjoying the feel of her silk dress rubbing against her soft skin. He lingered at the small of her back. While his tongue mated with hers, his hands continued their delightful excursion, moving down and cupping her firm round bottom, pulling her in until there existed no space between their bodies.

And now, she knew the extent of his desire for her.

She gasped and jerked out of his arms. The next instant, her palm connected with his right cheek. He didn't flinch. After the way she'd responded to his kiss, the slap was nothing more than a sting. Wouldn't even leave a mark.

Fury and confusion stared back at him, belying her dilated irises and her heavy breathing. She hadn't even put significant distance between them. He could easily reach for her again, but he knew that would be a mistake. What now? An apology would sound too insincere, but he needed to say something. Right?

She saved him the trouble. "Please leave."

Even her breathy voice told him things he shouldn't be hearing, told him the kiss had affected her more than she was willing to accept. He'd said she'd have to beg, but now, he knew he was going to do whatever it took to make that occur.

***

What just happened?

India blinked, staring after Omar, her mind wiped blank by his kiss. She stumbled back to the desk on wobbly knees and sank onto the chair. *Shameless.* She buried her face in her palms, still stunned by her reaction to him. She'd kissed him back, held on to him as if her very breath depended on it.

Her lack of restraint had revealed the truth to him, the truth she'd tried to hide when she'd sworn to his face never to yield to his charms. One kiss from him, and her body had made a mockery of her swaggering display of courage.

Her stomach growled, reminding her of the platter Omar had brought, the reason he'd come up in the first place. If she'd just taken his offer with gratitude as any sane person should, he might have simply walked off.

He'd been thinking about her wellbeing whereas she had been thinking...

She didn't know what the hell she'd been thinking, allowing him to stand so close that he could touch her. She nearly laughed. His sheer presence sent her heart into erratic rhythms, so his nearness had shattered any prospect of sanity she might have hoped for.

But she couldn't let this happen again. As much as the kiss had undone her, Omar still thought her capable of hiring someone to kill his brother. She couldn't allow herself to fall for a man who didn't trust her, a man who questioned her integrity.

***

Several hours later as she lay in bed, nerves kept her awake. She hadn't seen Omar since dinner, but she knew he'd come to bed, and—given that it was past ten o'clock—soon. Having no Internet or phone access, she'd spent the rest of the evening putting together a few new ideas for the Children's Foundation gala. Although it took place on the last day of the year, it was often called the New Year's Ball, since it ended after midnight, allowing patrons to usher in the New Year. Without the Internet to distract her, she'd been able to get a lot done.

She'd worked until eight o'clock when she'd decided to turn in, hoping to be asleep by the time Omar returned. However, without having work to focus on, her mind brought back memories of the kiss, and her body began to tingle all over again.

At close of eleven, the bedroom door opened, and Omar walked in. She froze, shutting her eyes. The carpet muted his footsteps, so she couldn't tell what he was doing until she heard the closet door slide open. He was humming a tune she didn't recognise, but the sound seeped steadily into her, heightening her already awakened awareness into chords of desire.

Curiosity propelled her to turn. She stifled a gasp as she noticed him undressing. The lights were off, but the open curtains allowed the moonlight to cast a gentle glow into the room, giving her an unhindered view of his silhouette. She swallowed, unable to take her eyes off. Even the muted lighting couldn't hide his glorious maleness. Heat engulfed her, and her breathing escalated. She'd been pressed against that body just hours earlier. What will it be like to feel him skin-to-skin?

He didn't appear to be aware of her observation as he grabbed a towel and wrapped it around his waist, then walked to the bathroom. He didn't shut the door, and the sound of the shower only increased her awareness of his nudity in there. Yearning pooled in a warm sensation between her thighs.

Several minutes later, when he emerged from the bathroom, she shut her eyes firmly, admonishing herself for being so affected by his presence alone. She stopped breathing as the mattress compressed under his weight. A few seconds elapsed.

"You're awake," he whispered.

His low, raspy voice had both a soothing and unsettling effect.

She sucked in a breath. "I thought you hadn't noticed."

"I've noticed everything about you since the first time I laid eyes on you," he said. "I also know why sleep eludes you."

"Oh?" She tried to sound casual, but another thought lingered at the back of her mind.

That first day. He'd felt it, too?

Was it significant? Did it change their current situation?

"You're thinking about me," he said.

His words should have sounded vain, but he delivered them in a matter-of-fact tone that dared her to deny them. She couldn't, but she refused to confirm them, either.

"Your silence speaks volumes, *ya jameel*."

She felt him move. The heat of his nearness surrounded her before his fingers brushed across her arm. She shivered in response.

"Turn around, *ya amira*. Look at me."

My queen, he'd called her. While this was technically a factual statement, she liked the way he said it. Then, she admonished herself. *Focus.* She didn't want to turn around and look into his eyes. Doing that had a way to scrambling with her thinking. Yet, when she attempted to speak, her voice failed to comply, so she saw no alternative than to oblige.

"There's no shame in admitting it. I've been thinking about you, as well," he said. "I've concluded that I must kiss you again."

He palmed her abdomen, causing sensual havoc with his gentle caresses. Her breath came in short, shallow bursts while the distance between them began to shrink.

"No." It sounded like a plea, and yet, she found herself adding, "Please."

"What are you afraid of?"

"This isn't about fear. How can you suspect me of treason and yet want to kiss me?"

He pulled back. "I don't see what one has to do with the other."

"It may not matter to you, but it does to me."

"Are you saying I cannot kiss you until your name is cleared?"

He'd put the words in her mouth, and they suited her, bought her time she needed to get used to all this influx of passions and desires.

"Yes."

"On one condition," he said after a moment.

"Name it."

"This remains a private arrangement between us. When we return to the palace, in front of my family and the public, we must keep the appearance of a happy couple in every sense for the benefit of my family."

She considered it for a moment. PDAs were largely frowned upon in many African societies, and Sudar would be no exception. Meaning he couldn't do more than a chaste peck on her cheek or lips. Certainly nothing that would lead to her being plastered against his body. Nothing she couldn't handle.

"Deal," she said.

"Goodnight, *ya amira.*"

His caresses stopped, and he retreated to his side of the bed, leaving her feeling abandoned, cold. How could she miss his touch when she'd silently pleaded for relief from the onslaught of desire he awakened in her?

More worrisome, though, was how quickly he'd conceded. Had their conversation gone exactly as he'd planned? Why did it suddenly feel like she'd just made a deal with the devil?

CHAPTER FIVE

Two days passed, and Omar had managed to keep his word. Not an easy feat considering she was his wet dreams personified. Despite waiting until late to retire to bed, she was always up, compelling him to acknowledge her, to talk. The more he learnt about her, the more he found himself drawn to her.

She wasn't just another princess, a socialite with a high regard for herself. He'd met enough of those. No. India had compassion, used her influence to raise funds for underprivileged children and women across the continent, and Sudar needed a queen with a heart like hers.

He found her in the sunroom, where she preferred to work. Personally, the brightness afforded by the tempered glazing in the large windows made the room too cheerful and distracting for work.

Standing at the door, his attention immediately caught on the movement of her sensual lips as she mouthed whatever she was reading on her laptop screen which was barely bigger than a standard iPad. The corners of his lips edged up.

After a moment, he cleared his throat, causing her to look up. For several seconds, he stared into her eyes, reluctant to start the conversation he foresaw would get ugly, but he'd never chickened out of anything, and he wasn't about to start now.

"How long have you been standing there?"

He took her question as an invitation in and entered.

"Long enough." His gaze swept over her simple black dress, worn with a small pendant on a silver necklace. "You look beautiful."

"Thank you," she replied. "I heard you picked my wardrobe."

He caught the disapproval in her voice. "Is there something you don't like about my choices?"

"Haven't you heard about colour?" Frustration marked each word. "Everything in my suitcase is black."

"As required by custom," he said. "A widow is expected to wear black for six months."

"What?"

He hadn't envisaged it to go down easy. It surprised him that she'd even waited this long to bring it up.

"There's an exception for inherited brides," he added. "You get to ditch the mourning clothes when you fully accept your new husband."

"Accept my new husband?" Her frown deepened, then cleared in a second. A gasp flowed out of her. "You mean...sex?"

He nodded and watched her bristle. She started to say something, then stopped. He could tell her mind had shifted to erotic territory when she avoided eye contact. As much as he'd like to dwell on sex, there were more important things to discuss.

"Take a break." He made sure his tone brooked no argument. "We need to talk."

To her credit, she didn't argue, but her curiosity was obvious. "I'm all ears."

He decided to cut to the chase. "We've been summoned."

She sat back, raised her brows. "I thought you did the summoning in Sudar."

"I do." Why did he find bantering with her so enjoyable? "However, officially, I'm not king yet, so my father still gets summoning rights."

"He wants you to go ahead with the coronation, doesn't he?"

"He does, but this isn't about my coronation," he said. "My father has come to know about your possible involvement in the accident."

Her expression immediately changed, her surprise metamorphosing into something he didn't want to name.

"He has 'come to know,' or you told him?"

"I didn't inform him, but if I came by that information, then so can The Crown."

"What exactly does he want from me?" she asked. "If he's looking for a confession, then he might as well join us here, because he's not getting one."

He tried not to wince at his next words. "My father insists on a formal interrogation."

"A what?" She pushed off her seat, her stoic exterior shattering. "This insult has gone on long enough. I'm India Aziza Saene, Princess of Bagumi. You do not hold me against my will, nor do you or your king get to drag my name through the mud."

There was hurt in her voice, anger in her eyes. Not unexpected. They still hit him like a punch in the gut. He remained calm, focused on diffusing her ire.

"The king simply wants your name off the list as do I."

"Tell me, Omar, who else is on this list of yours? Or are you simply looking for any scapegoat?"

"Look at it from his point of view."

"Is he looking at it from *my* point of view? Did he put you up to this?"

He raised his hands, letting her know he wasn't the enemy.

"Who's to say you're not holding me captive simply to buy time for your people to fabricate evidence against me?"

"I'm not trying to frame you. Trust me."

"Why would I trust you?"

"Because I believe you."

Silence followed. He hadn't meant to say that. Even though his gut instinct adamantly held on to a belief in her innocence, he'd planned on keeping it to himself until he had the evidence to support his credence.

"Then why are you doing this?"

"So I can interview you myself first," he said. "With enough information, I might be able to get him to back down. If not, then at least, when we leave for the palace tomorrow, you'll be ready."

***

India ignored her thumping heart and the apprehension that clawed at her. Although his initial accusation had been alarming, she hadn't taken it as a serious threat, assuming he'd been operating under the influence of his grief. The layers had fallen off now, allowing her to see the reality of the cruel joke that started with the appearance of kindness—giving her a place to recuperate.

He'd taken off the first layer of deception, revealing this hideaway home to rather be a detention centre, a blow he'd tried to soften by calling it a safe house. Now an interrogation? What would come next? Torture?

The dangerous thing about Omar was his charisma, the way he managed to manipulate her feelings to conform to whatever truth he wielded. Like a spy who pretended to be your friend while secretly extracting intelligence for his country. She'd fallen for it, too.

Even when she'd known the situation was bad, she had naïvely believed he'd be objective in his pursuit of justice. She'd assumed it would only be a matter of time before he found out the falseness of his accusations. It didn't help that her mental faculties seemed to glitch when he walked into a room, or that he appeared to know exactly how much he affected her.

"I need to get out of here."

"Where will you go?"

"Away from you." She failed to conceal her trembling in her voice.

He swore. "Are you afraid of me, India?"

She didn't respond. He tried to grab her as she walked past him, but she'd anticipated it and swiped her arm away just in time. She headed out of the room, through a short corridor leading to the dining room.

"We're miles away from anything."

The confidence in his tone only propelled her forward.

"Then I'll walk however long it takes to get to anything."

She broke into a trot as she heard his footsteps behind her. He called her name again, but she continued unperturbed.

"Come on. You've stayed here three days now. If I wanted to harm you, I'd have done it already."

Frustration seemed to bring out his French-accented "r." She must be crazy to notice it at a time like this. With firm determination, she shoved it out of her mind as she moved from the dining room, heading for the main door. Turning the corner to the living room, she screeched to a halt.

A bodyguard stood there—a buff man who looked menacing enough for her to hesitate. She'd forgotten about the guards. There was another stationed at the back entrance. She resumed walking.

"As your queen, I order you to let me pass." She issued the command with more confidence than she felt.

Behind her, Omar barked a command to the guard. "She does not step out of that door unless I say so!"

She stopped right in front of the guard, saw him hesitate, but ultimately, he seemed to take Omar more seriously. She shoved him. He didn't budge or bat an eyelid as his gaze focused straight ahead.

Suddenly, Omar was upon her, his hand closing around her upper arm.

"Release me at once, Omar!"

As she attempted to wriggle out of his grasp, he flipped her around in a manoeuvre as fluid as a dance move, and the next thing she knew, he'd arm-locked her, holding her hands in a firm grip behind his shoulders. She fought back.

"Stop fighting me, India."

His hold remained strong, preventing her from breaking free, but loose enough that she didn't feel crushed by his strength. He gave her room to wiggle, but suddenly, the more she moved, the more her body became aware of his in a purely carnal way. She stopped struggling. Her already quickened breath didn't slow down.

He released her hands, and instead, wrapped his arms around her. His expression softened as he crushed her against him. Her hands, which were now splayed against his solid chest, didn't appear interested in pushing him away. *Traitors.*

"You're not in any danger here," he said. "You know that, right?"

She tried to respond, but her suddenly dry lips didn't move. She licked them, hoping to get them to cooperate. His gaze dropped to her lips, and she knew what was coming.

"You're going back on our agreement," she said in a low voice meant only for his hearing, but her gaze darted to the guard. "We only have to kiss and hold hands in front of your family."

"I said in front of my family and the public," he replied. "He's the public."

It was such a silly line, she shouldn't let him get away with it, but before she could speak up, he added, "Unless my wife deems the staff to be insignificant."

Amusement lit up in his eyes. He'd effectively tossed her into an incongruous situation. She either had to declare the guard to be inconsequential or accept Omar's logic and give in to his kiss. She swallowed. It would go against every grain in her body to dismiss the guard. *"Everyone has a station in life, but no one is more human than another."* Words her father used to say when she was growing up echoed in her head, marking the moment her mind registered that she had to concede defeat.

With no further protest from her, he captured her lips. He didn't tease or coax, didn't have to. The moment their lips touched, passion swept her. She allowed him entry, responding with ardour as if their first kiss had never ended and this was simply a continuation. He was possessive yet gentle, demanding and giving all at once. As their tongues duelled, her hands clawed his chest, grabbing tufts of his garment in shameless gratification of the sensations he unearthed in her.

She'd been kissed before, but not like this, not until her body lost awareness of self. These were new sensations, a reaction unique to Omar, and she was lost in them.

When he pulled back, her breath came out in rapid puffs.

"If you hit me again, know that I'm going to kiss you once more until you're too aroused to move or even think."

Excitement galloped up her spine at his seductive threat. With jellified legs barely holding her up, she was already close to not being able to think, but she'd rather have her teeth pulled out than admit it to him.

"I have more restraint than you give me credit for."

The thickness of arousal echoed in her voice.

"And I have more fortitude than you give me credit for, *ya jameel*," he said with quiet determination. "I'll clear your name and claim you as my wife in every sense."

She shivered. How was he able to arouse her desires so easily?

"Now, shall we get back to the business of the mock interrogation?"

***

The study was officially India's least favourite room in the house. She'd only been in here twice, and neither occasion had been pleasant. Once again, she sat on the leather sofa facing Omar. This time, however, he didn't distance himself. Instead, he pulled up a chair and sat across her.

Though seated, he didn't appear less imposing in any way.

"Tell me about the accident," he said.

"I've already told you about it."

"Tell me again."

She huffed but narrated the events once more. When she was done, he remained silent for several moments, his brows furrowed.

"With whom were you communicating?"

"I can't tell you that."

He gave her a pointed look. "You cannot refuse to answer any question. The crown interrogator will not be lenient."

She raised her chin in a show of defiance. "If that's all it takes for them to convict me, then so be it."

He let out a sigh. "Your text message said, 'abort. M Not alone'. What did that mean if not you calling off a hit because the target wasn't alone?"

"It wasn't."

She'd known him barely six weeks, maybe seven. His low opinion of her shouldn't matter, but it did. She mentally pushed passed the sting, steeled herself against further surprise emotions threatening to break free.

"Can you at least tell me what the message meant?"

She remained quiet, debating how much she could tell him without compromising someone else's safety.

As if he could read her mind, he said, "If you're trying to protect someone, I can help you, but not if you withhold information from me."

A gut instinct urged her to trust him. Could she put any stock in it when that same feeling had made her stay here for three days instead of running? If he was serious about helping, however, she could use the assistance. A woman and her little girl's lives depended on it.

"My work with the Children's Foundation isn't only about throwing parties and raising funds to help underprivileged women and children." She paused, taking a deep breath. "We also fund rescue missions, helping women escape from abusive domestic situations."

He released a slow breath, his brows creased. "That's a dangerous undertaking."

She nodded.

"More so when there are children involved." After a beat, she added, "So now you know why I can't tell you details."

"Are you personally involved in these rescue missions?"

"No." If the topic hadn't been a dire one, she'd have found humour in his question. "We have people working for us. Professionals. Soldiers for hire, if you want."

His expression relaxed, but only a fraction. "Was there a rescue planned for that day?"

His tone had lost its hard edge, and she got the feeling he'd veered off the original path of this mock interrogation.

She clasped her hands together, nodding. "Things weren't going as planned."

They hadn't heard from the soldier helping them at the stipulated time, and her partner, once a military nurse, had wanted to go on her own. India's quick message had been to deter her from walking into a dangerous situation without the necessary protection.

"I've never told anyone about this aspect of the work I do. Not even my family." The enormity of what she'd just done propelled her to grab his hand. "You can't discuss this with anyone."

"Couldn't you use your position to get these women the refuge they need?"

"In some cases, yes, especially in Bagumi, but our operations go beyond our borders," she replied. "Some of the abusers are powerful and well-connected men. If they knew who was behind their wives' freedoms, it would put many people's lives in danger and create an international incident."

She bit back the sickening feeling at the pit of her stomach that suggested she'd just made a huge mistake. "Give me your word that you won't repeat this to anyone."

His brows furrowed. "You have it."

She let out a breath she hadn't realised she was holding and released him.

"How did you get into this?" he asked.

It was a fair question, and the answer might help him keep his word.

"During my undergrad studies, I discovered my roommate was being sexually abused by her step-father. Her mother was a housewife with no income of her own, so although she knew about the abuse, she continued to stay with the man. She tried to protect her daughter by sending her to a boarding school when she reached secondary school, but she still had to endure abuse during vacations. I invited her home one holiday, and it sort of continued from there. I had her mother's blessing, and she could visit with her daughter when she wanted."

"Did her step-father not fight this?"

"He never officially adopted her, and since her mother had given consent, Marianne stayed with us until we graduated, then she found a job."

Anger burned in his eyes, though it didn't show when he spoke. "Did she have siblings?"

She nodded. "A younger half-brother. The apple of his father's eye. He was safe."

"What happened to her mother?"

"She passed away three years ago, but she stayed with her husband until then."

Stunned at how comfortable she'd felt confiding in him, she prayed she'd done the right thing. Omar was an enigma. They had a connection, something she hadn't experienced with anyone who wasn't a blood relative. Yet, she couldn't ignore the fact that he'd married her while she was in a coma. Who did that? Nor could she discount the accusation he'd levelled against her, even if he'd told her moments ago that he believed her.

"I'm sorry about your friend," he finally said. "Are you still in touch?"

She nodded, smiling as she thought about her friend's incredibly optimistic outlook on life despite her past. "Marianne is now a successful lawyer based in Accra, Ghana. Her firm specialises in domestic abuse cases."

Several seconds elapsed with neither of them speaking.

After a moment, he spoke. "Can I ask you a question?"

She nodded.

"Did you love my brother?"

She blinked, taking several seconds to reorient her mind. She hadn't seen it coming at all. Was that a trick question? Why did she sense there could be no right answer to it?

Choosing her words carefully, she replied, "I only met Majid five times before we were married."

"Nevertheless, did you fall in love with him?"

Her heart became like lead in her chest as she shook her head.

"I'm sure he was a good and honourable man," she explained, hoping to soften the blow. "Perhaps, in time, we might have grown to love each other."

He released a breath.

"Thank you for your honesty." He stood, slipping his hands into his pockets. "Do you need time to mourn him?"

She gulped. There might be no right answer, but there was a slew of wrong ones, and she feared any response might fall into the second category, so she threw his question back at him.

"What about you? Don't you need time to mourn your brother?"

"I've accepted the cruelty of his passing," he said. "I'll do him a greater honour by finding and punishing his killers."

His resolute expression didn't fully mask the grief in the depths of his eyes. She wanted to make him a promise to also honour his brother's memory by living, but it would be hasty. Omar still didn't trust her. He might say he believed in her innocence, but was that enough? Was it unrealistic of her to want him to take her at her word?

CHAPTER SIX

There was something about the Sultan's Palace—the official residence of Sudar's royal family, as well as the headquarters of the monarchy—that took India's breath away. That was saying something, since she'd lived her entire life in one of the most beautiful royal residences in the world—the Royal House of Saene.

Situated on a hill in the heart of the capital city, M'Bamina, it was visible from many parts of town. As they drove through the merlon-decorated white walls, she gazed at the extensive French-style flower gardens flanking the long drive and surrounding the castle.

"Beautiful, isn't it?"

Omar's voice cut through her thoughts.

She turned. "Yes. You have a stunning home."

He nodded with pride. "I've lived here thirty years, and yet, the view still doesn't get old."

It wasn't just the drive up and the gardens. The building itself—a unique blend of medieval, traditional Sudano-Sahelian and modern architecture—had its walls embedded with stunning African motifs dominated by nature images interspersed with geometric abstractions. She'd been in awe on her first visit.

"How old is it?"

"The original structure dates to the fifteenth century, and some of it still stands today. But Sudar has had a chequered past, and some rebuilding and additions have been necessary over time."

"We're using the formal entrance," she noted.

"Yes. We both have official duties to perform this morning. I thought it wise to get them over with before lunch."

Trails of uneasiness pulsed through her, despite the logic of his response. His sunglasses shielded his eyes, barring her from reading his expression, although the stern lines of his lips gave her a fair idea of what to expect.

She didn't know how many people were privy to her real status as an unwelcome guest in Sudar, but she braced herself for a hostile reception. Although the king had been friendly and even fatherly during her first visit nearly two months ago, today, as a grieving father looking for someone to hang, she couldn't expect the same treatment.

Realising her hands were balled into fists, she released them, smoothing out her black trousers with nearly invisible pink stripes before resting her hands on her lap. If he noticed her nervousness, he didn't comment. After all, he appeared to be preoccupied.

The car came to a stop, and the driver got out and opened the door. She got down after Omar. A uniformed palace staff met them, offering a bow and a greeting. They acknowledged the staff's greeting.

The main door opened into a foyer where a small welcome party awaited them. She schooled her expression as her gaze clashed with that of Omar's mother who stood with his sister, Faridah, on her right, and Janae on her left.

India breathed a discreet sigh at the sight of Janae's familiar face. Even though they'd only spoken once, she'd had good vibes about Omar's young aunt. Her gaze returned to Faridah, whom she'd met twice before, if she excluded the wedding day. Her mocha complexion glowed against the vibrant colours of her sheath dress made from African wax-print fabric. She stood slim and model-tall, her round face bearing a striking resemblance to their mother.

India eyed the colourful outfit while missing her usual wardrobe. *You can change that tonight.* It was a voice in her head, but it sounded like something Omar would say. All she had to do was give in to her desire and sleep with him. She nearly winced as she pushed the thought out of her mind and brought her attention to the present.

Omar embraced his mother. "*Kayf halik, ya'umi?*"

"I'm fine, *ya walidi,*" Queen Azmera said, then she turned to India. "Sudar has three official languages—English, French and Arabic, but my son has always been partial to Arabic."

India nodded. "I've noticed."

Warmth enveloped her at the memory of the endearments he preferred to say in Arabic. She made a conscious effort not to look at him and risk having the warmth turning up her body heat any further.

"Accept my condolences, Queen Azmera," she said, extending the sympathies to the others by looking each of them in the eye. "May you find comfort for this great loss."

"Thank you, India. You may not have known Majid long, but you've suffered a loss, too," she said. "Let no one make you feel your grief is inferior to ours."

Sudden tears prickled her eyes. Sometimes, it was hard to believe how much had changed in the span of less than two months.

She blinked, trying to reel in the moisture and her surprise at the queen's words. "Thank you."

The queen's eyes watered, too, but she blinked and cleared her throat.

"We Sudari are known for our resilience," she said, her voice surprisingly steady. "Yes, my heart bleeds for the son I've lost, but I also rejoice for the daughter I've gained and pray for the happiness of the son who still lives."

As Omar embraced his mother again, India couldn't help the tug in her heart.

Pulling back, the queen regarded her son with a smile. "Speaking of your happiness, I hope you haven't forgotten about the gala on Saturday night. I'm glad your father managed to talk you into coming back today instead of Friday like you planned."

"A party isn't necessary, *ya'umi*."

"We have a duty to celebrate new wives, but even more so an inherited wife." As she said this, Queen Azmera turned to India.

Janae, who hadn't spoken since they walked in, spoke up. "Besides, it is important for the royal family to show the people of Sudar that their leadership is still strong."

"It is what Majid would have wanted," Faridah added with a vigorous nod.

Omar turned his gaze to her, his brows raised askance. "If India is okay with it."

She nodded. "We'll be honoured, Queen Azmera."

"Excellent, because you're the guests of honour." The queen then faced Omar. "Your father awaits you in his study. We'll keep your wife company."

Omar leaned in, and she held her breath while he brushed a kiss on her cheek, leaving her body tingling.

"You'll be shown to your office afterwards. I'm sure you're eager to get in touch with your family."

India nodded, welcoming the news that she would be back online soon. She had a lot of catching up to do.

"See you at lunch," he said. "For now, I leave you in the able hands of the queens of the castle."

"There's only one queen here," Faridah said. "The rest of us are divas. Know the difference, little brother."

"Little brother?" Omar said. "We're back to that?"

"I didn't realise Faridah was older," India said.

"By an entire week," Faridah replied, still smiling at Omar. "Now that you're would-be king, you need to be reminded even more."

The others laughed, but India frowned, not catching the joke.

"I don't understand—"

A short, awkward silence followed. Had she said something wrong? The other women looked at Omar, whose expression had turned unreadable.

"My biological mother, my father's junior wife, died in childbirth," he said. "Queen Azmera had given birth only a week before, so she nursed me alongside Faridah. She's the only mother I've ever known."

"And I love you as much as my own children," the queen added, embracing him.

Something twisted in India's chest, something that made her heart ache for Omar. Watching them, she had no doubt about the love mother and son shared, and yet, she couldn't help wondering if he ever missed the woman he'd never met. Would her life have changed anything about him?

"Queen Shaida was a good woman, well-loved by the people for her great contribution to our dear kingdom," Queen Azmera said after she'd released Omar. "Even though I'd have loved to see my Majid live and become king, I'm happy Shaida's son gets this honour."

"Thank you, *ya'umi*,"

The atmosphere remained heavy after he left, and as much as she'd have loved to say something to break the ice, something else preoccupied her mind. Were the women aware of Omar's suspicions? Nothing about the way they'd welcomed her suggested they did, which made her believe Omar and his father had kept the news to themselves. She hoped it remained that way. There was no telling their reaction if they found out. Either way, she'd be irresponsible if she allowed herself to be lured into a false sense of security. She needed to keep her guard up.

***

Omar couldn't decide which was more ridiculous. The fact that he'd spent the past four days with one of the world's most beautiful women without making love to her, or that he was beginning to fall for her in that short span of time and despite the lack of intimacy.

Truth, unfortunately, couldn't be denied. Why else would this unquenching desire to vindicate her cling to him when he was her accuser? Why did a part of him wish he'd kept the information to himself until he had more to go on? It would have been one way to go, but he'd needed to see her reaction first hand, hear her side of the matter, let his instinct gauge her sincerity.

He also hadn't abandoned the possibility of her being a potential target, which meant he still needed to do all he could to keep her safe, including continued monitoring of her messages and calls. An act that would surely piss her off if she found out. *Best not to let that happen.*

First on his agenda, he needed to talk his father out of the formal interrogation and allow General Khaya to uncover the evidence required. Discretion was key. If he had his way, this thing would go away quickly. The longer it took, the higher the risk of the rest of the family finding out. He wouldn't want to put her through that.

If he couldn't talk his father into standing down, then he'd have to ensure the interview took place in a secret and secure location. Even that posed its set of problems, not to mention the implications for ties between their two nations. And to his marriage, which had yet to begin in the proper sense, a situation he intended to rectify as soon as possible.

He pushed that delectable thought out of his mind in favour of focusing on the business at hand. Pleasure would have its turn later. Just before entering his father's office, he sent a message to General Khaya summoning him to the palace for a briefing.

When he reached the door of this father's study, he stowed the phone into his breast pocket and knocked on the door. The study had become the outgoing king's new office since relinquishing official duties to Omar.

The old man sat at the desk cleaning his collection of tobacco pipes. Even though he'd quit smoking many years ago, he still collected pipes and diligently cleaned them from time to time, particularly when he needed to relieve stress.

"Baba," Omar said.

His father looked up. "Come in. Sit. We have much to discuss."

Omar hadn't expected a short or easy meeting, and as he took a seat opposite the older man, he braced himself for a tough discussion.

He studied the worry lines on his father's forehead. "What is it, Baba?"

"How was your honeymoon?"

"It wasn't a honeymoon," he replied. "India needed rest. I made sure she got it."

"I don't know if I should be proud or disappointed to hear that."

He frowned. "Why would you be disappointed?"

"It doesn't matter right now." His father waved a dismissive hand. "You promised to keep me posted on the investigation, and yet, I had to find out about your only suspect through my own sources."

"I said I'd keep you apprised of any important developments."

"You think finding a suspect isn't important?"

"The evidence we have is circumstantial at best. Given whom it is we're pointing fingers at, we must be a hundred percent sure. Until then, I wish you'd allow me to conduct my investigation the way I see fit."

A few seconds passed.

"Then you'll be happy to know I've decided to hold off on a formal interrogation."

Relief filled him, but he didn't let it get to his head. It was only a postponement.

"This doesn't mean I won't question her myself. I need to look her in the eye and ask her a few questions."

"I already did, Baba. She's not involved."

"You're her husband."

"What difference does it make?"

"I've seen the way you look at her. I assume you find her desirable, which makes your opinion biased."

"My desire to avenge my brother supersedes everything."

"What about your coronation?"

Omar raised his brows. "What about it? What could be more urgent than finding Majid's killer?"

The worry lines on his father's forehead became even deeper. "Your uncle means to challenge you for the throne."

He blinked. "What?"

As the story went, his father's only brother, Latif, had hoped to become king when several years of marriage between King Rafael and Queen Azmera had yielded no heirs. Majid's birth had derailed his aspirations, and the subsequent addition of Omar had moved him from second to third in line. His father had appointed him Emir of the state of Umm Jafar and given the state a semi-autonomous status. This power seemed to have satisfied his uncle, but recent allegations of corruption and tyranny in Umm Jafar had brought negative PR to it as well as the throne.

"When I gave him Umm Jafar and oversight of its neighbouring regions, I thought I'd put a leash on his ambitions for the throne. I was wrong."

"He didn't challenge Majid. Why is he challenging me?"

"There was no question about Majid's ascension, but the unfortunate turn of events creates a loophole that plays in his favour."

"In other words, he thinks I'm an easy target." His clipped voice revealed his opinion about it. "I'd like to see him say it to my face."

"This needs level-headedness, Omar. If he were challenging you to a physical fight, we wouldn't be having this conversation, but the fact that you haven't fulfilled all your marital obligations gives your uncle a foothold."

"I've spent the past four days alone with India. Uncle cannot be certain I haven't touched her."

"You didn't marry her under normal circumstances, and he knows as well as I do that you're an honourable man who will give his bride the chance to mourn her first husband."

He mulled over his father's words, which felt eerily like the old man had been listening in on his and India's last conversation.

"In any case," his father continued. "It won't matter, because, if Latif makes it official, you'll have to swear on the Sacred Stone. You may be able to bluff before the Council or even beat a lie detector, but you can't do the same with the stone unless you want to invite misfortune upon the entire kingdom."

Sensation seeped out of Omar's limbs as the gravity of his father's words hit home, rendering him momentarily speechless.

The Sacred Stone was believed to have fallen to Earth from the Heavens many centuries ago during the Great War of Succession. The stone had been summoned by a sorcerer, Amon, to decide between two feuding families who should rule over Sudar. The stone whirled toward Earth in a ball of fire, and upon collision with the earth, created a blast that had consumed the wrongful claimants and their supporters, thus bringing an end to a war that had been raging for nearly eight years. The El Dansuri clan had ruled the kingdom since.

He'd always thought the story had simply been legend until he'd been shown the stone upon turning eighteen. The sorcerer had been buried beside it, ensuring that their combined powers would continue to protect Sudar and its royal lineage. He still didn't know if the stone truly had powers, because they hadn't had to consult it in nearly a hundred and fifty years.

"If your uncle becomes king, the kingdom will suffer for it." His father's expression was regretful. "I hate to push you, Omar, but you must put honour aside for the sake of the kingdom, and time isn't on your side."

Omar cursed. His father's request meant going back on his word to India, unless he could resolve the case within that time.

He'd always known about the time constraint, which under normal circumstances shouldn't have come into play. The royal constitution required succession to happen within six weeks. India's hospitalisation had cut that time by two weeks, which, added to the four days, meant half of that time had already expired. Consequently, he had three weeks to bed his wife or risk losing his claim to throne.

Getting her to bed wasn't the problem. From her responsiveness when he'd kissed her, he knew he'd only have to push a little to get her to yield. The question was, did he want to be that guy? Seducing her into submission might have a nascent appeal, but he wanted this marriage, wanted India more than he'd desired any woman before. There could be no regrets when they finally made love.

He'd just have to find a way of avenging Majid and thwart his uncle's plans without going back on his promise to her. If the Sacred Stone had any true power, it would know Uncle Latif would be a bad choice for king, even if technically, he ticked all the boxes.

"There's more," his father said. "If you haven't made her your wife in the true sense by the time the grace period ends, and your uncle becomes king, he'll have the right to also lay claim on her."

Rage slammed into him.

"This is exactly why I went ahead with the inheritance rites when I did, and you're telling me it may all have been for naught?" The mere thought of his uncle even thinking of India, let alone making a claim on her, made bile rise to his throat. "Like hell he will."

Forget the Sacred Stone. He'd like to be left in a rink with his sleaze ball of an uncle and have the decision made by the power of their fists. He was usually not given to irrational feelings and behaviours, but as anger mushroomed within him at his uncle's audacity and outright disrespect, rational thought was steadily vacating his senses.

"Omar, *'iihday*," his father's voice reached him. "Calm down."

Omar sucked in a breath, trying to calm his heart, which continued to beat as one possessed.

"I promise you, Baba, I'm going to settle this thing once and for all."

With that, he excused himself. By the time he stepped out of his father's office, he'd managed get a hold of his emotions. He hadn't shed his anger, though. He'd reeled it in and put a cap on it, intending to redirect it to better use.

CHAPTER SEVEN

Omar waited until he'd reached his office where he could make a call on a secure line. Seated at his desk, he dialled General Khaya's number.

"I have another suspect for you, General," he said when the call was picked.

"Yes, Sire?"

"The emir of Umm Jafar."

"Your uncle?"

If he didn't know the general as well as he did, he'd have missed the hint of surprise in the man's voice. They had investigated everyone who stood to benefit from Majid's demise, including Uncle Latif who was now next in line for the throne until Omar produced a successor.

The thought of making an heir brought on images of India and the exploration he'd like to execute on her curvy body, the sounds she'd make when he finally had her moaning and writhing with pleasure. He squelched those thoughts and brought his mind back to the conversation.

"I've received new information that warrants a thorough look at him."

"If I may ask, Sire. Are you able to disclose the nature of this information?"

"My uncle intends to challenge me for the throne, so no matter the outcome of our first investigation, he's now the number one suspect in my book."

"Yes, Sire."

"And, General? Don't leave any stone unturned."

"Of course not, Sire."

After the call ended, he buzzed his personal secretary. "Moses, is Uncle Latif coming to the banquet?"

"I'll check the confirmed guest list, Sire."

"Very well."

Clicking off, he sat back, contemplating his next move. If his uncle was coming to the palace tomorrow, then he might be planning to make his declaration known then. If so, Omar needed to be ready, which meant he had to spend his time between now and then coming up with his counterattack. Something that would nullify the threat before it became one.

***

Nearly two hours after their arrival at the palace, India finally got a moment alone. The ladies of the castle had given her a partial tour of the work areas of the palace as well as the ballroom for the dinner dance, which was in a flurry of activity as staff prepared for the occasion.

They had then settled in a regal tea room where Queen Azmera, Janae, and Faridah had taken her through some Sudari royal protocols as well as new duties she'd be taking over after Omar's coronation.

At the end of the tea meeting, the queen had summoned Salma who'd arrived promptly and escorted India to her new office. It was a large space, decorated in soft hues of beige and brown, which provided a perfect canvas for adding her own personal touches.

She now sat at her desk in an executive chair that felt so comfortable, she worried she might fall asleep in it.

"If I may say so, My Lady, you look refreshed," Salma said. "It was good His Royal Highness insisted on whisking you away for a few days."

"Thank you, Salma. I do feel rested."

"His Royal Highness appears to care a lot for you." As soon as the words were out, Salma's eyes widened. "I'm sorry, My Lady. I didn't mean to be so bold."

"Don't worry. I expect my staff to be comfortable around me." India smiled. "If you'd met Amal, my previous assistant, she'd tell you I don't demand all the formalities."

"Thank you, My Lady."

"I also like to know about the people I work with, so why don't you tell me about yourself?"

"There isn't much to know about me, My lady."

India smiled. Having gone through this process many times, she understood the other woman's hesitancy. However, once they overcame the initial hurdle and got to know the woman behind the princess, they relaxed and gave off their best.

She motioned for Salma to sit. "Why don't we start with how long you've worked with the royal family?"

The PA seemed to hesitate a moment before taking the seat.

"Six years, My Lady."

"Do you like working here?"

"Oh, yes," came the response. "Everyone is friendly, and the pay is good. It's the only way I could afford—"

She stopped abruptly.

"Afford what?"

Salma's entire body language screamed this was not a topic she wanted to get into. India decided it best not to push.

"Do you have family?" she asked instead.

After several moments of silence, the other woman nodded. "I have a sister."

"That wasn't so bad, was it?"

Salma shook her head. There was no mistaking the relief that spread across her face.

"Good. I need to catch up on emails," India said. "I'll alert you when I'm done."

Having dismissed Salma, she could finally play catch up. Aside from the phone conversation with her father after waking up from the coma, she hadn't had contact with her family. Added to the past four days of having been cut off from technology, she was eager for some parts of her life to get back to normal.

Her computer bag sat on the desk. She whipped out the laptop and booted it, then opened a browser in incognito mode. This was a standard precaution she took when dealing with matters concerning any rescue mission, but it was even more important now, since she suspected Omar or his father would be tracking her calls and emails.

Disquietude settled over her when she went through all her inbox and didn't find anything from her partners. She sent a coded email which would not mean much to anyone who intercepted it. She'd hoped not to risk making a phone call, but she needed to know her partner hadn't put herself in any danger. She'd give them twenty-four hours before taking that risk.

An email from Amal regarding the theme for the Children's Foundation Ball made her smile. They had decided on a masque ball. Since India liked to use the occasion to promote new designers, Amal had sent a list of four relatively new names in the industry who were interested in making her outfit. After a quick Internet search of each designer, she bookmarked the search for future attention.

Funny how little interest she had in picking out a dress when that had been a huge deal three months ago. A lot had happened since then. She'd married, been widowed, been inherited by her late husband's brother, been accused of treason by her new husband…been kissed by him. Her skin tingled at the memory of those kisses.

She shook them off. Her body and mind already worked overtime in his presence; she didn't need to add unsolicited thoughts of him when she was alone. Their last kiss had brought her on the brink of rescinding her condition for allowing him to make love to her. What did that say about her resolve? She needed reinforcements, and she knew exactly who would give her the needed boost.

Picking up her cell phone, she dialled her sister Isha's number. If anyone could sympathise with her, it was her older sister. Like her, Isha was also to enter a marriage alliance. As their mother's older daughter, she should have married first, but Sudar's succession rules had time constraints that had dictated India's wedding date.

The phone rang three times before being answered. "Look who finally decided to call her sister?"

She smiled. "Good morning to you, too."

"How are you?" Concern had replaced her sister's earlier jovial tone.

"Physically, I'm fine. It's a miracle I got away with minor scrapes. Mentally, it's a lot to process, but I'll heal."

"How's Omar?"

India took a few seconds to consider the question. "He's adamant about avenging his brother."

"I can't imagine what he must be going through. When I heard about the accident, the thought of losing my sister made me rethink so many things."

She had to ensure the conversation didn't take an emotional turn. "How are preparations toward your wedding?"

"You know, the standard fairy-tale wedding."

"Your enthusiasm is staggering," she teased. "Seriously, I'm glad you didn't take my accident as a sign to walk out of the marriage alliance."

"I thought about it, believe me, but I realised walking out would be selfish. Life is too short for that. Besides, like Baba says, great privilege goes hand-in-hand with sacrifice."

She nodded. "It would be a different story if we had found love and eloped like Amira."

"Wishing for love? I take it Omar doesn't float your boat?"

India gasped. "Is sex all you think about?"

"Now why would you say something like that?"

She lowered her voice as she responded. "You gave me a vibrator at my bridal shower."

A robust laugh drifted over. "In case your husband disappoints. I was simply being a good big sister."

"It was embarrassing."

"Come on, India. You aren't still upset about that, are you?"

Isha lived for pranks. As Bagumi's Minister of Trade, her negotiation skills could charm the pants off anyone, but she could also put you in a tight corner if she wanted to. That present amid their mother and aunties had been a deliberate act to put India on the spot.

"I'll decide after I pay you back in kind." A chuckle broke through her attempt to make her voice stern.

"I'm always a step ahead, sister. After twenty-six years, you should know it by now."

India shook her head, sighing. "It's great talking to you."

"Me, too, but I have to run," Isha said. "Sorry. I'm speaking at a Diamond Exhibition conference in Johannesburg in two days, and I haven't packed."

"Okay. I'll talk to you later."

"Sure thing."

Several minutes after ending the call, she still had a smile on, imagining the general excitement of another royal wedding in Bagumi. The citizens loved royal functions, and weddings were only surpassed by royal births.

While thinking of royal functions, she found her mind drifting to Omar. What would it have been like if he'd been the one from the start? Her heartbeat quickened as she remembered his heated gaze, and before she could stop herself, she'd opened a web browser and typed his name in the search window.

It didn't surprise her that the first result was about him taking over from his brother. That and the accident were the main stories from international news sources. The result that caught her eye, though, was number eight in the list—an article from a site called *African Royals Unlimited*, known for their sensational headlines and tendency to stretch the truth. She should know better than to pay heed to anything they had to report, but she couldn't resist when she read: *Sheikh Omar El Dansuri's Legitimacy in Question?*

She clicked on it, carefully reading through a lengthy piece discussing the old requirement of full Sudari parentage for kingship and how it was changed, but not much on why this affected Omar's legitimacy. The article dedicated several chapters to Sudar's male-preference succession system, which put Omar ahead of his sister Faridah.

She sat back contemplating it. Evidently, she was the only one who didn't know Faridah was older, and even after she'd learned it earlier, she hadn't put two and two together. If Faridah had been male, *she* would be the heir apparent instead of Omar.

Sudar appeared to have some archaic traditions that didn't sit well with the feminist in her. History had produced formidable female leaders across the world, which should be enough proof that women could hold such positions of power with positive results. In Bagumi, females were raised to be just as fearless as males. The urge to do something about the situation gripped her, but she held no real power in Sudar; not until she became their queen. She sucked in a breath, realising what it meant. She had to remain married to Omar.

Her phone rang, its sound piercing through her thoughts. She sucked in a breath, calming herself. The caller ID made her pause. *Private Number*. Finally, an update. She swiped the screen.

"Hello."

Silence met her response.

She frowned. "Hello?"

The sound of breathing drifted across the line. An ominous shiver slithered up her spine, and she cut the call. Heart racing, she stared at the phone. Was this a crank call, or had someone managed to discover the person behind the rescue missions? Could she be in danger?

You're getting ahead of yourself, India. She'd always made sure to take all necessary precautions whenever she'd dealt with a rescue, and she'd never been personally involved in a mission. She left that to the professionals. This was nothing to worry about.

Why, then, did her heart still beat like someone was on her tail?

A knock on the door caused her to start, and the phone dropped with a loud thud on the desk. The door opened, and Janae peered in. India released a breath.

"Can I come in?"

"Please."

Janae entered and shut the door. "Are you okay? For a moment there, you looked like you'd seen a ghost."

"I'm fine." She forced a laugh and hoped it sounded convincing. "How can I help you?"

"You mean, how can *I* help you?"

India arched her brows up, her interest piqued.

Janae winked, raising a gift box. "I come bearing gifts."

"Gifts?"

Janae sat on the two-piece chaise sectional, the only other seating available aside from the visitor's chair. She placed the box on the coffee table and unwrapped it to reveal two generous pieces of chocolate cake. India's mouth instantly watered.

"You're a woman of your word."

"I don't joke when it comes to chocolate." She winked. "Are you going to stay there, or are you going to join me here?"

She didn't have to be asked twice. Pushing back from her chair, she stood and walked around the desk to the chaise.

"You need to sample this before you ruin your appetite with lunch."

She chuckled. "Isn't it the other way around? You're spoiling my appetite for lunch?"

"Believe me. You want to eat this while you have space in your stomach."

Janae stood and walked over to the cabinet on the opposite side of the room, returning with two saucers. She placed a piece of the cake on one saucer and handed it to India before serving herself.

Her eyes twinkled with eagerness, causing India to chuckle as she took the saucer.

"It looks good." Dark and rich and moist.

"Tastes even better."

She bit into it. "Oh, my."

"Right?"

She shut her eyes briefly, moaning shamelessly as she savoured what had to be the best chocolate cake she'd ever tasted. It was moist—so moist—and scrumptiously melt-in-your-mouth chocolatey.

Janae echoed her moan as she took a bite of hers. She was right. It would have been a shame to fill her stomach with lunch before having this little piece of Heaven. As she took in her second bite, her mind drifted back to the time Omar had fed her the chocolate cake and their sizzling first kiss. This time, her moan was definitely not in celebration of chocolate.

As though her mind had invoked him, the door opened, and Omar entered, immediately snagging her attention. She nearly choked as she swallowed. He stopped a few steps away from them, directly facing her. He glanced briefly at his aunt before returning his attention to her.

"I see you're getting my wife into this bad habit of yours, Aunt Janae."

"Trust me, she's already a believer."

He gave a snort of laughter. "Good to know."

Her tongue sneaked out to moisten her suddenly dry lips, and his gaze zeroed in her mouth.

"I'm afraid something has come up, and I won't be able to join you for lunch."

"Oh?" she said.

"I'll make it up to you at dinner."

He looked at her as if he wanted her on the menu. She shut her eyes, cutting herself from his penetrating stare. All she managed to do was invite images of herself as the main course on his *carte du jour*. Her eyes flew open, found him still focused on her. Was that amusement in his gaze?

Without another word, he turned and walked out. Only then did she remember she hadn't been alone in the room. She swallowed, licked her lips again, and composed herself before turning. Janae stared at her, one brow raised in the exact manner as Omar.

"What?" India asked.

"When you came back wearing black, I assumed you hadn't packed anything else. I didn't realise you two haven't..." She hooked her two forefingers and wiggled her brows.

She tried to ignore the fire burning her cheeks. "Wh—what makes you say that?"

"He still has the predator look of a man who can't wait to pounce, and you looked like a deer caught in a car's headlights," Janae replied. "The tension between you two? Wow."

India popped the last piece of the cake in her mouth to avoid offering a response.

Unperturbed, Janae continued. "Either you're not a red-blooded female, or my nephew isn't as charming as they say he is."

India only smiled. Omar was definitely not lacking in the charm department, except when he was accusing her of crimes she hadn't committed.

"You do find him attractive, don't you?"

The frown on Janae's face gave India pause. The other woman's persistence reminded her of Isha, and even though she knew next to nothing about her, India felt at ease with her.

"I wouldn't be a red-blooded female if I didn't."

"He is good-looking, isn't he?"

"So was Majid."

She nearly winced. Why the hell did she say that?

Janae looked at her for several moments, her expression contemplative. "I want to tell you something."

"Okay."

"I have a friend who lost her husband a year after being married. They had a new baby, and her family had very little, so going back to her parents would have put undue pressure on their finances. She accepted her brother-in-law's offer to take her as his wife." Janae paused as if waiting for her to fully absorb what she'd said.

"I didn't accept Omar. I woke up to find myself already taken without consent."

"I know, and you need to talk to him about it," Janae said. "Especially if you think you might develop feelings for him."

"Love and feelings have no place in my marriage," she replied. "I understood that from the moment I accepted to be a part of the marriage alliance with Sudar."

"Don't be so sure." Janae took her hand. "You see, my friend and her first husband had a cordial relationship, but when she married his brother, she fell in love. In the beginning, she couldn't get past her feelings of guilt. She feared she was dishonouring her first husband's memory by falling in love, especially with his brother."

India swallowed but did not offer a response. This hit too close to home, although not for the same reason.

"I don't know how you felt about Majid. My guess is, unless it was love at first sight, then you probably didn't know him long or well enough to have developed feelings for him. Either way, don't beat yourself up if you find yourself falling in love with Omar."

India released a breath, still unable to decide how to respond to Janae's assessment. She didn't know about falling in love, but she couldn't deny her attraction to him. How did she tell the other woman that the issue wasn't that she felt guilty for being more attracted to Omar than Majid, but that she didn't feel guilty enough?

What would Janae say if she knew what her nephew had accused his wife of? Would it change her advice? She had no answers to those questions, but she knew one thing for sure. As long as he didn't trust her, falling in love with Omar was out of the question.

CHAPTER EIGHT

What did his uncle want? That question had plagued Omar's mind since his father had told him about Uncle Latif's intention to challenge him for the throne. If his uncle hadn't openly opposed his father or Majid's potential assumption of the throne, then why now? He hadn't been able to figure out an answer, which was why he'd spent the past forty-eight hours developing a plan of action.

Thus why he was in his office on Saturday instead of home with India. By the time he'd finished briefing General Khaya and his team, it was already six-thirty. That left no time to return to the residence to shower and change. Thankfully, his office had an adjoining bedchamber with an en-suite bathroom and a closet with several changes of clothes.

After a quick shower, he changed into a stylish jodhpuri suit his sister had bought him on a trip to Dubai last year. It was the only formal black outfit he had aside from tuxedos, and he wore the latter only when he had to. Call him biased, but he'd always found a certain extra elegance in non-Western attires.

Heading out, he met Moses at the door of his office.

"Sire, I have a message from Her Royal Highness," he said. "She'll meet you at the base of the stairs in front of the banquet hall."

"Thank you, Moses."

Omar reached the foyer at the base of the stairs. She wasn't there yet. Good. It wouldn't have been all right with him if he'd kept her waiting. From the sounds of music and chatter reaching him, it appeared the pre-dinner cocktail was in full swing. Taking in a deep breath, he mentally refocused, determined not to let on about what was really going on, especially since his uncle was attending the event.

He sensed India's presence and looked up. Just like the first day he'd set eyes on her, everything in him went completely still, his only awareness being of her as she took a first step down the stairs. Her neck-high, black silk dress embraced her curves up to her waist and flared gently to her feet where a gorgeous golden thread work beautified the hemline. Draped over her shoulders, a see-through fabric with crystal embroidery glittered when the lights hit them. The full effect gave the appearance of her floating down to earth.

Completely immersed in the vision of her, he forgot to move as she took the last step, which brought her within inches of him.

"You're staring," she whispered.

Her voice had gained a sensual, breathy quality. He liked it. A lot.

"Kunt takhudh 'anfasi baeidana, ya amira."

She smiled. "What does that mean?"

"You've never asked the meaning of anything I've said in Arabic before."

"I understood the others, but my Arabic is limited."

"I said, you take my breath away, my queen."

He didn't add that he wanted to whisk her back to their residence, peel off her stunning fashion ensemble, and make passionate love to her. All of that would have to wait until he could get her to trust him, but it didn't mean he wouldn't steal a few kisses tonight.

"You look handsome," she said.

"Thank you, but I assure you every eye is going to be on you tonight, including mine." He offered his arm. "Shall we?"

Her gaze faltered a fraction, exposing, for a couple of seconds, unbridled desire, the intensity of which staggered him. She blinked, veiling it, and hooked her hand through his proffered arm.

They were announced as they entered the banquet room, and all eyes turned to them. He led her through the crowd, pausing intermittently to shake hands with guests. Finally, they reached the far end of the hall where his parents stood.

His father raised a hand, and a hush fell over the room.

"It gives me great pleasure to welcome you all to the queen's dinner dance. As you know, my family, and indeed the entire kingdom, has suffered a great tragedy, which is still raw for many of us. However, I don't want today to be about tragedy. Let us rather celebrate life."

A round of applause exploded around them.

"It also gives me great pleasure to introduce for the first time my son, Omar, and his new bride, Princess India Aziza Saene of Bagumi, as the would-be-king and queen of Sudar," his father continued. "And now, if you would all follow me, I believe dinner has been served."

Omar was glad for all the experience in diplomacy he had because his impatience would, otherwise, have surfaced. All he wanted to do was to get the festivities over with and be alone with India. It was a dangerous desire, but he'd risk it for even one kiss. He refocused his mind on the present as they filed out of the room.

The guests were ushered to their seats by the banquet hall staff.

"We're not sitting together?" he inquired, noting the seating arrangements.

"No, my dear," his mother said. "This is not a wedding reception. Don't worry. You can have her back after dinner. You two are opening the dance floor."

He tried to ignore his annoyance, but the thought of having her in his arms later lightened his mood significantly. He didn't kiss her as he'd have wanted. Instead, he gave her hand a gentle squeeze and pulled out her chair. She thanked him and sat down.

"*Bon appétit*," he said.

She grinned. "*Merci*."

His gaze lingered on hers for a few second before he turned and was led to his table. Luckily, the seating arrangement, while unfavourable, placed India within his line of vision.

She appeared completely at ease seated between two portly diplomats who seemed unsurprisingly enthralled with her. He forced his attention back to his table, smiling at his companions.

Dinner was a three-course affair that tried his patience as he spent the next two hours making small talk. Every now and then, his gaze trailed over to India who smiled graciously at the diplomats while chatting. Everyone at her table, including the females, appeared to be hanging on to every word coming out of her lips.

He shook his head. A room full of more than two hundred, half of whom were females—beautiful females—and he had eyes for only one. He couldn't seem to stop staring at her. As though she sensed his attention, she glanced up. For several seconds, he lost awareness of everything else as his gaze zoned in on her lips, which curved into a slight smile.

His heart seemed to expand and contract. *Ya'Allah,* he had it bad. Somehow, he managed to return his attention to his table and participate in pockets of conversation.

After dinner, the party moved back to the banquet hall. The cocktail tables had been repositioned to create space in the centre of the room, which had been transformed with the lighting of the crystal chandeliers and an orchestra set up.

The royal protocol officer drew guests' attention. "Distinguished ladies and gentlemen, Their Royal Highnesses, Sheikh Omar and Princess India, will now open the dance floor."

The moment he had been waiting for. An excuse to have her in his arms.

He held out his hand. "Would you honour me with the first dance?"

"It will be my pleasure," she replied.

Leading her to the middle of the floor, he slipped his right hand behind her, resting his palm on the small of her back. He pulled her closer than was strictly standard as the music started. His gaze never wavered from hers as he led her through the smooth steps and turns.

She glided, executed each step, each slide, each turn with exquisite elegance. Every brush of their fingers felt like a jolt of electricity powering his heart and his desire.

"You dance beautifully," he said.

"As do you."

He'd always enjoyed the waltz, but never more than today. Whatever brand of magic she wielded, she had him ensnared, and he didn't want to be released. Without having rehearsed, they moved in sync, as though they were always meant to do this. Would they be this compatible when they finally came together as one?

When the music eventually ended, applause rose from the guests. A new tune stole in, an invitation for others to join in. A tap on his shoulder yanked him out of the demi-trance resulting from staring into India's eyes.

He turned and froze, unprepared for the sight meeting his gaze.

"Uncle Latif."

"Omar." His uncle, standing eye-to-eye with him, gave him a smile that didn't reach his eyes before turning to India. "Will the princess honour me with the next dance?"

Omar pulled himself together, masking his displeasure with a smile of his own. Various ways of declining passed through his mind, none being suitably appropriate. In any case, the assent wasn't his to give or deny.

"Of course, Sheikh Latif," India said, setting the distaste in his mouth.

He relinquished his hold on her. "I can only be apart from her for one dance, Uncle."

His choice of words was intentional, aimed at debunking any notion his uncle might have about the status of Omar's marriage. If Uncle Latif thought his nephew had been intimate with India, it might cure him of his aspirations for the throne.

"You're generous," his uncle said. "In your shoes, I might not be able to live up to such high standards."

He made a conscious decision to disengage. Although the knowledge of his uncle's intentions made it that much harder. However, he'd already resolved to defeat the man to an extent that would deter him from ever eying the throne or India again.

***

India's gaze followed Omar as he retreated to the side-lines. She missed his arms already. What was happening to her, and why did his effect on her seem to only grow stronger? From the moment she'd reached the top of the stairs and found him waiting at the base, she hadn't been able to think straight. The appreciative look in his eyes and his compliment had only served to fan the flames of her desire.

"He'll be back soon enough," Uncle Latif said, bringing her attention back to the dance.

"Forgive me, Sheikh Latif."

He shook his head. "There is no shame in desiring one's husband."

She did not wish to speak about her desires for Omar with his uncle, so she decided to change the subject.

"I trust you had a smooth journey to M'Bamina."

"I did."

As they moved in a circular motion, her gaze found Omar. He was staring at her, his eyes narrowed. He looked exactly as Janae had described him. *The predator look.* She sucked in a breath.

As the song ended, he started advancing towards them. Her heart began to race, then dropped when a woman intercepted him, curtsying in a manner that meant only one thing. An invitation to dance. With a glance her way, he bowed and took the woman's hand.

"It must be my lucky day," his uncle said.

She ignored her disappointment and fell back in step, but her gaze inexorably trailed around seeking Omar. She always found him staring right back. Heat swirled around her insides, and need forked through her, turning her yearning into liquid heat between her thighs.

"You mustn't worry about Omar spending time with other women," Omar's uncle said. "I can assure you my nephew is more bark than action."

She disliked Sheikh Latif. The negative vibes she'd picked up the moment he'd tapped Omar's shoulder intensified, and his latest comment solidified the impression. Still, she couldn't help wondering about the meaning of his words. Could he be referring to the investigation? Had Omar or his father voiced their suspicions—however erroneous—to Sheikh Latif? Could she trust Omar to work in her favour?

"Wisdom comes with age," Uncle Latif continued while executing his dance steps with mechanical skill, but lacking finesse. "I believe older men make better husbands. You see, young men need time to tame the hunter in them before they settle down."

Her heart thumped with an angry tempo, but she needed to be tactful . "You don't think your nephew has tamed the hunter in him?"

"I'm too much of a gentleman to drag another man's name in the mud, let alone the next ruler of Sudar," he replied with an irritatingly smug smile. "What's a mere mortal to say when the gods appear intent on blessing a man who five decades ago wouldn't even have been eligible for the throne?"

Years of training in public etiquette and social graces saved the day. Otherwise, she'd have frozen on the dance floor or missed her step in her attempt to pick up her jaw from the floor. She forced the corners of her lips up, pretending he hadn't just dropped a bomb. Omar not eligible for the throne? Why did this question of eligibility keep coming up?

The smug smile remained on his lips, indicating her cool exterior didn't fool him. He raised her hand, initiating a spin. She turned and found herself facing Omar. Unbidden joy rippled over her being. Without another word, Sheikh Latif relinquished his hold, and relief washed over her.

The reprieve was short-lived as the heat and tingles returned full-blast the moment Omar's hand closed around hers. The intensity of his gaze stole her breath.

"Come with me," he said.

There was an urgency to his voice that compelled her to follow him without protest until she realised they were headed towards the door.

"Where are we going?"

"Somewhere more private."

She stopped. "Why?"

"I'm going to kiss you," he replied. "Long and hard. We can do it here or somewhere more private, but it's happening."

Excitement thrummed through her. There was no denying it. She yearned for him, despite his accusations against her. Inside, her head warred against her heart. Was she sending an unintended message by following him? Could she separate her physical wants from her emotional need for his unwavering trust?

A few minutes later, they stood on a balcony overlooking one of the many palace gardens, surrounded by the susurration of its water fountain. The balcony was unlit and far enough from the banquet hall to provide the assurance of privacy. However, lights from the garden afforded some illumination.

He pulled her into his arms. Given the extent of her yearning, she should probably run. She didn't. Her need for his embrace and his kiss superseded caution. They were out in the open, so nothing more than heavy duty kissing could take place. Surely, she could handle that without feeling like she'd compromised or gone back on her word.

"Your lips have beckoned me all evening," he whispered. "My desire for you overwhelms me tonight."

She'd expected him to capture her lips the moment they were alone. Instead, he continued to hold her close, caressing the exposed skin on her back. Shards of pleasure spiked through her. She found herself wrapping her arms loosely around his waist, leaning closer.

"You overwhelm my senses, too, Omar."

"Then why do you fight your desires, *ya amira*?"

The low rumble of his voice washed over her, making her insides shudder. His lips were inches away, his breath a gentle breeze over her face.

"I'm not fighting now."

He grunted. His hands moved up, sliding slowly over her waist, lingering on the outer edge of her breast. She sucked in a breath, her chest rising and falling with her long and heavy breathing.

"How far will you go, my queen?"

As if to test her, his thumb grazed over her nipple, and a sharp sensation jolted within her. She knew exactly what he was asking. Would she allow him to make love to her? The dampness of her panties as her inner muscles quivered screamed yes. Recklessness and caution fought for dominance. What if this was just an act for him? A game? Charm meant to break down her defences just to get what he wanted.

"I'm not ready for that, Omar," she said. "Nothing has changed. You're still investigating me."

"Only to prove your innocence," he said. "Is it not enough that I believe you? Can you not take me at my word that I will clear your name?"

"What if you never uncover the truth?"

"Then I'll die trying."

Her breath whooshed out of her, echoing with surprise. His lips, now only a breath away, beckoned. Her eyes began to shut as the wall of her resistance came tumbling down.

Someone cleared their throat, forcing reality to pierce through the moment. Omar pulled back a fraction, not looking at the intruder.

"Sire?"

"Leave us!" he said between clenched teeth.

She couldn't see who had interrupted them as Omar shielded her from the entrance, but whoever it was didn't appear to be leaving.

"I'm sorry, Sire, but you want to hear this, before you draw the curtains on the day."

Omar shut his eyes for several seconds before pulling back. He took in a deep breath and exhaled slowly.

"I'll walk you back to the banquet hall," he said to her.

She shook her head. She was too aroused, too off-balance to go back to the party and pretend Omar hadn't just unravelled her without one kiss.

"I'd rather retire now."

"Asobo," he called, and one of his bodyguards appeared. "See my wife to the residence."

"Yes, Sire."

His expression had hardened, as had his voice; so much in contrast with the gentleness of his touch and whispers a moment ago. He'd shifted from lover to ruler within the twinkle of an eye while she stood by still reeling.

What did it mean? *Love*, her mind provided. Her breath hitched. *Oh, God.* Could she be falling for Omar?

CHAPTER NINE

To ensure utmost privacy, Omar didn't speak until he and General Khaya had entered his office and shut the door.

"This better be good, General," he warned even though he knew the older man wouldn't otherwise have interrupted him and India.

"It depends on which side you stand, Sire."

"Tell me, at least, that you have enough evidence to go against my uncle."

"We have still not found any indication to suggest your uncle had anything to do with the accident."

"Look harder."

"My men are still on it," the general said.

"Good. I've enlisted Faruk's help. I understand my uncle is spending a few days in M'Bamina, which gives my cousin the perfect opportunity to investigate. With him on the inside, we'll surely find what we need to take my uncle down."

The general nodded. "I can confirm that Sheikh Latif does intend to make his challenge formal before returning to Umm Jafar."

"I'm ready for him," Omar said. "But you didn't interrupt me and my wife to tell me this."

"No, Sire. Given the new information about Sheikh Latif, we took a second look at all the possible suspects. We dug deeper and further in time. Text messages, phone records, CCTV footage, where available. We uncovered some new information." General Khaya shifted. "You won't like this."

"Nevertheless, I must deal with it."

The general pulled something out of his pocket and held it out. It looked like a mini-recorder.

He steeled himself to the potential damning response, which he'd already been warned about. "What's that?"

General Khaya pressed a button on it, and the room filled with a voice distinctly India's.

It has to look like an accident.

No. For several seconds, he disbelief immobilised him, shook him to the core. He turned, taking deliberate steps to his desk, and sat down.

"Where did you get this?"

"We hacked into the phone provider's database," the general answered. "We've run it through audio forensic tests. Without a good exemplar, we can't be a hundred percent sure, but we are significantly certain it is the princess consort."

"She isn't involved."

"If I may speak freely, Sire," General Khaya said. "You may not want it to be true, but you have to entertain the possibility just to avoid the element of surprise."

After a moment, he moved. "Leave it on the desk."

General Khaya did as ordered. "I will see myself out."

Omar didn't respond. Instead, he picked up the recorder and played it again. And again. And again. He knew she'd kept part of the story. She'd said as much. But this was a damn important bit to leave out.

Pushing himself off the chair, he swore. He'd gone from burning for her to boiling with anger. He inhaled deeply, attempting to calm his racing heart, to assuage the rage directed at her. Surely, there was an explanation for the tape.

Either that, or he'd fallen for the world's best actress. He needed to confront her, but not in this state. In a few minutes, though, after he'd brought his emotions back to rational levels, he would, and she'd better told him everything.

***

India managed to hold herself together until she'd entered the main door. Thanking Asobo and his colleague, she dismissed them. Once inside, surrounded by silence, she let out the breath she seemed to have been holding since leaving the balcony. The heat of his touch continued to sear her skin, making her burn with need.

Why do you fight your desires? His question rang in her ears. She was afraid. Pure and simple.

His maleness which attracted her and gave her wet dreams, his kisses that turned her into a mass of needs and wants. Her actions tonight had revealed exactly how much he affected her. She desired him with a fierceness she hadn't known she possessed, a ferocity that made her want to be his in every sense of the word. Yet, the truth remained that he still thought her capable of something horrendous.

Even with this knowledge, the fire he'd ignited continued to smoulder and inflame her passion. All she wanted now was to turn it off. The constant stream of a cold shower would do just that. Hopefully, she'd be asleep before he returned.

She took off the shawl and let the delicate fabric slip through her fingers onto the ottoman at the foot of the king-sized bed. Next, she unzipped her dress and shrugged it off, shimmying out of it until it lay in a pool at her feet. Since the dress had been open-back, she hadn't worn a bra, so she now stood wearing only panties. Finally, she rid herself of her those, as well.

Oh, yes. She inhaled deeply, held it, and released it in one long breath. Removing the encumbrance of clothes already brought relief. She picked up the dress and laid it by the shawl on the ottoman. The panties would go into a laundry basket in the bathroom, so she left it on the bed and headed into the walk-in closet for one of her nighties.

What she wouldn't give for a girls-night-in with her sisters. Girl-talk often helped whenever she anxiety threatened to invade. However, she couldn't infringe on Amira's honeymoon, and she didn't need any of Isha's teasing. Not in her current state.

Maybe tomorrow. Right now, she craved that shower. She retrieved a soft blue nightie whose lace flowed like soft waves. Thankfully, she wasn't restricted to black when it came to sleepwear, and this happened to be one of her favourites.

She sighed. What was she still doing in Sudar? The plan had been to leave as soon as she found a way of escaping her imprisonment without jeopardising the treaty. Now, her feelings for Omar were jumbled up, making her want to stay a little longer. She shook her head. What was she thinking? If tonight had taught her anything, it was that she and Omar weren't on the same page. May be not even in the same book.

A thud snapped out of her thoughts, and she searched around for what she'd dropped. She gasped upon seeing the gift box, which she explicitly remembered *not* packing. *Isha, what did you do?* She knew its contents. Her face heated as her mind drifted to the hasty bridal shower her sisters had insisted on holding for her, how the others had laughed while she'd sat there wondering what her sister had been thinking.

In case your husband disappoints. She snorted. Omar's kisses promised things she had yet to imagine.

A worrisome thought occurred. What if he found her limited experience a disappointment? She swallowed.

Curiosity propelled her to open the box. Maybe she could use the vibrator to gain more experience. She stared. She could at least take it out and read the instruction manual. *No harm done.* She sat on a pouf in the closet, took out the satin pouch, and retrieved two objects. A round one with a battery compartment, which she gathered was the remote as indicated on the box. The other was a portable, bullet-shaped object about the length of her middle finger but thicker and attached to a string. *The vibrator.*

She shook her head. Omar's latest antics had her wet and aching, but she didn't need this. What she needed was a cold shower and not an orgasm.

Just as she was about to replace it, a shadow darkened the entrance, causing her to jump. She looked up, and her gaze clashed with Omar's. He stood at the entrance, looming. He stepped in, and the closet seemed to shrink around him. As she scrambled to stand, the box fell, spilling its content. With horror, she watched the remote roll towards him, stopping only when it collided with his shoe. A shiver ran through her as he knelt to pick it up.

"When you said you're not ready, what you meant was you aren't ready for me," he said in a scarily calm voice, his eyes blazing with anger and hurt.

She only managed to shake her head. "It's not what you think."

"Isn't it?" He paused, his gaze sweeping over her as if her nudity had just occurred to him. Her body reacted as though a flame had been lit inside her. "This looks like a device that operates what you're holding."

He rolled it in his hand, and the bullet vibrated in hers. She jumped again at the unexpected sensation. Her nipples contracted into tight aching peaks, and her intimate muscles quivered.

"That's what I thought."

Her heart thudded as his icy glare shot another shiver up her spine. She should be scared, and she would have been if she didn't also see passion brewing underneath.

"I can explain."

He pinned her with his gaze, and whatever she'd meant to add got stuck behind the lump that had suddenly formed in her throat. She eyed her clothes, wishing she could pull at one to cover herself. As if reading her mind, he moved in farther, putting himself between her and her clothes.

"My uncle means to challenge me for the throne."

"What?"

He gave a dry laugh. "If he does, the only way I win is if I've fulfilled all the requirements for ascension to the throne."

The information made her reel. Could he seriously lose his claim to the throne? Wasn't he the automatic heir?

"You said it would suffice that we shared the same room."

"Not if I'm challenged." His voice had dropped an octave, sounding angrier with every word. "So now, I can't have my coronation because I haven't slept with my wife. Meanwhile, she won't sleep with me because she prefers a machine to the real thing."

"Please, let me explain."

"I don't need explanations, India!" he snapped.

A little cry escaped her. Why was he so angry? If he'd just listen. This was undoubtedly due to the news that had warranted an interruption of their time on the balcony. What could be so bad that it would take him from passion to ire in such a short period?

"I do want something, though."

"Wh—what?"

"Since you're putting on a show, I'd like to watch."

She gasped. "Omar, please, I can't—"

"It's either that, or I march you out of here and straight to my father, and you can tell him why I haven't been able to set a coronation date."

Her eyes widened. "You wouldn't do that."

"Wouldn't I?"

"I don't know what's upsetting you, but you're jumping to conclusions, Omar."

He didn't seem to be listening at he marched over to the few clothes she'd taken out and hung up. He picked one and threw it at her.

"Your choice. You either do it while I watch, or you put on the dress and we head out."

"You would do that to me? To a woman you say you desire?"

"I was wrong about you. You're not the woman I thought I desired. You don't tell the whole truth, and you keep secrets. You're just the woman I had to marry because of a treaty between my country and hers."

His words, his impassionate tone, cut her. Whatever feelings he might have been developing for her seemed to have vanished, or he couldn't see beyond his fury. Either way, she had no doubt he'd see his threat through.

"You need to calm down."

He rubbed his forehead as of his head suddenly ached. "It's been a long day for me, India. Make up your mind."

"I—"

"What now?"

"Would you execute punishment without mercy?"

He snorted. "I gave you two choices, India. Mercy wasn't one of them."

Several charged seconds elapsed as they stared at each other. She'd been fully aware of her nudity, but she became even more conscious of it, of her vulnerability. She wanted to run and hide—yet, an indignant part of her wouldn't allow her to take the coward's way out. He wasn't prepared to listen to her explanation, which meant she had only one viable option. There was only one problem with that.

"I—I haven't used one before." Her voice cracked under the weight of shame.

There was a pause after her admission, and she prayed he was reconsidering.

"Fine. Give it to me. I'll insert it for you," he said.

"Omar—"

"I won't ask again, India."

After the passion they'd shared earlier this evening, his coldness stunned her, wounded her. However, the fact that he still jumped to conclusions without giving her benefit of a fair hearing hurt more.

She blinked back imminent tears, silently dropping the gadget into his open palm. As she walked past him, their gazes met, thrusting her back to the banquet, to the moment when he had taken her hand and said he was going to kiss her. Threads of exhilaration zapped her.

"Get on the bed."

His voice had turned husky, and she realised he was affected, too. She affected him. Why didn't he just admit it, then? The answer hit her immediately as she recalled his words from a few days ago. He wanted her to beg. The realisation infused her with an odd sense of dominance.

When she reached the bed, she lowered herself onto it, then lay flat on her back.

He came to stand at the foot of the bedstead. "Open up."

She parted her legs, anticipation thrumming through her. He came to kneel between her legs, and she held her breath, waiting for his caress. He only touched her long enough to spread her thighs wider. Doubt crept in, knocking down her confidence a peg or two. If he truly wanted her, wouldn't he fondle or tease?

"You're so wet." The intimacy of being naked and exposed before him should have been the most romantic thing; yet, he spoke as if he'd made a scientific discovery.

Shame engulfed her as she realised the error in her assumption. He didn't want her. The discovery didn't diminish her own desire. Even the brief touch of his hands had intensified her ache and need for release. With fingers at the apex of her thighs, he parted her folds. She shivered, stifling a moan. With her senses already heightened, her body primed, the hardness of the vibrator touching her opening caused a quiver of her intimate muscles. She tensed.

"Relax, *ya jameel.*"

His voice washed over her, the endearment causing a calmness to settle over her.

"Good girl."

He eased the gadget into her, and as it settled into place, a shock of pleasure zapped her. Having completed the task, he stood, her centre on full display to him. *What next?*

"Is it comfortable?" he asked.

Not sure she could engage her voice, she nodded. The next moment, he pressed the button, and the vibrator hummed inside her, emitting a gentle pulse. She jerked. A moan left her. She closed her eyes briefly, absorbing it.

She met his gaze. His eyes had gained that intense look he got when he was about to kiss her, but aside from that, he appeared unaffected as he played with the remote, regulating the vibes and pulses while she whimpered and squirmed.

"Omar."

It came as a moan. A sharp increase in the vibrations wrenched a pleasured cry out of her. Her hips gyrated as she tried to contain the sensations. Her fingers grabbed the sheets. Her breasts had become heavy, their peaks aching. She found herself yearning for his touch. No matter how good this felt, it didn't compare to what she'd experienced in his arms.

She tried to sit up. "Omar, please…"

The intensity increased again, cutting off her plea. She cried out, falling back. He never took his eyes off her as he controlled her body, dictating her pleasure without touching her. By denying her his touch, he'd ensured that it would be all she wanted. Yet, she couldn't reject the intimacy of staring into his eyes as her body experienced erotic sensations from his actions.

His name tumbled out of her again and again. She writhed, her breathing erratic as pressure began to build inside her, winding her tight like a coil. Despite his impassive stance, she saw the rise and fall of his chest. Watching her turned him on.

With that realisation, the coil snapped, releasing waves of rapture. They engulfed her. She cried out, her hips jerking off the bed, her back arching up, then she tumbled back. She whimpered and purred until her breath returned to normal. Her eyes fluttered open, met his hard gaze.

"Omar."

He cut her off. "Let me know when you want to do this again."

He flung the remote across the room, and as it dashed against the wall, the impact activated the vibrator, triggering a second orgasm. He began to walk away, and her heart shattered amid her cries of release.

***

Omar had no idea how he'd managed to leave a naked India on the bed and make his way to the living room where he now stood nursing the sting of her rejection—the cherry on top of the cake of a failed day. He was no closer to avenging his brother, and he'd still not found a viable way of preventing his uncle from challenging him for the throne. Not unless he slept with India. Finding out she'd rather satisfy her needs with a toy than ask him cut deeper than his other failures.

And that damned tape kept echoing in his head. What was India up to?

His mind drifted to the precious moments when he'd had her in his arms on the balcony, willing and pliant. Had he been too aggressive? Had he somehow scared her? Had he driven her to this?

No. She hadn't acquired the toy between then and now. She'd always had it.

He cursed.

He was rock hard, aroused to the point of pain, his body trembling slightly in protest to his resistance. There was no way he was going back in there and making a further fool of himself by begging her to have him.

He may have physically removed himself from the bedroom, but his mind remained there, unable to shut out images of her naked form, her lush curves, her softness, her passionate moans. When she'd mentioned his name, it had almost broken him. *Ya'Allah*, she'd looked exquisite against the sheets purring and writhing, staring at him as though she'd wanted him.

He swore again and clenched his fists, making a conscious effort to push her out of his mind. As he began to gain a modicum of control, he decided it best to take a shower and go bed. A good rest would help him to regroup. He wouldn't achieve either by lying next to India, so he retreated into one of the other rooms.

Taking off his clothes, he walked into the bathroom, turned on the shower, and let the cool water pelt him until he was drenched from head to toe. It did nothing to deflate his erection. If he was going to have sound sleep, he needed to do something about it.

Fuck.

Rubbing soap in his palms, he contemplated an act he hadn't resorted to in ages.

India.

He may not have gone on his knees and begged, but she'd still brought him to his knees.

He closed his hands around his shaft and shut his eyes. Images of India poured into his mind, images of her nails digging into his back the way they'd dug into the sheets; of her body clenching around the vibrator the way he wanted her muscles to grip him. A harsh groan sounded in his throat. He could so easily have taken her, sunk deep into her hot wetness and lost himself. He wanted her. *Ya'Allah*, how he wanted her.

He couldn't have her, though. If and when they made love, it would be with her explicit consent. There could be no grey areas when she finally succumbed, so today, he used his imagination as he brought, to his body, the relief it needed.

Renewed anger burned in the pit of his stomach when he finally turned off the shower. He was the biggest idiot amid all humanity, because despite her rejection, he'd die trying to clear her of any suspicion.

CHAPTER TEN

Over the next three days, India focused on work. With the gala getting closer by the day, the last thing she need was to dwell on Omar, even if that seemed to be the only thing her mind wanted to do.

The morning after the banquet, she'd woken up alone, breathing a sigh of relief because, between wantonly exposing her need for him on the balcony and what inadvertently happened later, she hadn't thought she could face him again. Thankfully, two families feuding over land rights had forced him to take a trip out of M'Bamina, giving her the much-needed space to focus on anything other than him.

Or so she'd thought until he'd called to check in the moment he'd touched down at his destination. The past three days, he'd called every night before bed, ensuring she'd carry him over to her dreams. Damn him.

This morning, with twenty-four hours until she had to face him again, she'd decided to focus on speaking with potential sponsors. The organisers did the ground work, but when it came to the special cases—celebrities and corporate bigwigs, who needed assurance that the foundation was real or any number of other reassurances—her name and title came in handy, so she'd volunteered to handle them directly.

"Yes, the Children's Foundation advocates for mental health," she assured a potential donor, a wealthy widow who insisted her donation had to support mental health in memory of her son.

Through their initial email communications, she'd sensed the woman would need a little special attention, which was why she'd set up this video call. Listening to the story about the woman's only son's recent suicide made her heart ache. Since the cause was so personal to the woman, India further assured her she could request for a financial statement of her donations as well as the Foundation's audited financial reports, which were public record.

The call ended with a pledge amounting to the second highest individual donation they had received so far this year and the purchase of a full table—ten tickets—for the end of year gala.

After writing down the details, she pushed the paper forward to Salma who had been helping her to update the list of special case donors.

"One more call, and we'll be done for today," India said.

Salma didn't respond. Instead, she stared at the laptop screen, her fingers idling on the keyboard, showing no indication of having heard the comment.

India snapped her fingers. "Salma, are you okay?"

The mention of her name jolted the PA to attention. "Sorry, My Lady, I was just—"

"A million miles away. Is something the matter?"

"Nothing, My Lady. I didn't know you were an advocate for mental health."

The delivery of the words struck a chord, and she knew instinctively that it wasn't a passing comment. It was personal.

"Salma, if you need to talk to someone, I can help."

"I'm fine." She shook her head. "It's not me."

"Someone you know?"

"My sister." She paused. "It's not that bad. She has good days and bad days, that's all."

"And today is a bad day?"

Salma nodded and blinked away tears. "I'm sorry."

Unable to stop herself, India rose and went around the desk to Salma's side, placing her hand on the other woman's shoulder.

"She's your sister. It's not nothing, and you don't need to apologise for it."

India grabbed some tissue from a box on her desk and offered them to Salma, who took it and dabbed her eyes.

"Thank you, My Lady." She blew her nose.

India should probably take a few mental steps back. How many times had her mother warned her not to get too familiar with the staff? However, she had never been able to see another woman in distress and simply walk away. A blessing and a curse.

"She was so beautiful, so full of life and love." She gave a snort. "Love. It makes us do incredibly stupid things."

India's heart went to her. "It does."

"You understand?"

She nodded. "Perhaps not in the sense you mean, but I'm here in Sudar because of my love for my kingdom and for my father."

If she were being honest, there might also be a part of her that thought she could—or feared she would—fall in love with Omar, but she wasn't going to think about that.

"Then maybe you're lucky, My Lady. Yours is the unavoidable kind of love. My sister fell for the wrong man, someone rich and well above her station."

"You don't believe love conquers all?"

"No, My lady. Not the love of a man, anyway. My mother used to work for their family. That's how they met." She'd pulled herself together now, but it appeared once she'd started, she couldn't stop. "He told her he loved her, filled her head with lies, and she believed him. Eventually, his father found out about them and forbade their relationship. My mother lost her job."

India said the only thing that came to mind. "I'm sorry."

"You asked if she's having a bad day." She shook her head. "It's been a tough month, since she heard about his wedding. You see, he broke her heart and married the kind of woman his parents approved of."

Several seconds elapsed. Emotions clawed at India as her heart ached for a woman she'd never met. If she felt this way, then Salma must be feeling so much worse.

"We're done here for now, so take a few minutes while I catch up on my emails."

Salma nodded and murmured another thank you before heading out. When she opened the door, Moses, Omar's PA, stood there poised to knock. A flurry of tingles overcame her, forcing a sharp intake of breath. Moses had been part of Omar's entourage for the trip. Did this mean what she thought it meant? Had Omar returned a day early?

As Salma hastened past Moses, India gestured for him to enter.

"Good morning, My Lady," he greeted with a bow. "His Royal Highness requests your audience."

She released a breath and hoped he didn't notice the combination of nervousness and excitement the mention of his boss evoked. At the same time, a flame of annoyance sparked within her heart. Who the hell did he think he was, summoning her?

After what happened, and after proving, once again, his willingness to jump to conclusions about her, she had no desire to accept his summons. She recognised, though, that her fight was with Omar and not his employee, so she nodded.

"Lead the way."

Walking through the corridors connecting the various offices and reception rooms, she distracted her mind by admiring the intricate African motifs that gave a nice appeal and character to the décor. When they reached Omar's outer office, Moses led her straight to his door and opened it while announcing her arrival.

As soon as she entered, her gaze found Omar seated at his desk, wearing a navy-blue power suit with a striped blue and gold tie. He looked delicious.

He sat back, his gaze lazily roving her body from head to toe as if undressing her in his mind. Her body heated. She tried to ignore the fact that he'd seen her naked, but the closest she'd come to seeing him in the nude was watching his silhouette drawn against the window on a moonlit night. She barely registered the door shutting behind her as her mind fetched the memory.

"Good morning," he said, jolting her back.

She shoved the image out of her mind. "I thought you were returning tomorrow."

"We managed to come to an amicable solution early this morning. I didn't see the need to delay my return."

Had he been eager to see her? Had he been thinking about her the same way her mind insisted on dwelling on him? Squelching the thought, she reminded herself that she was pissed with him.

"You asked to see me?"

He stood and motioned her to a seat.

"I'll stand," she said, hoping to convey her disinclination to be in his presence longer than necessary.

"Sit down, India. It's not a request."

She folded her arms and gave him her most defiant look. "And if I don't?"

He stared her for a couple of seconds before letting out a heavy breath. "Suit yourself."

His quick concession dented her confident exterior, but she squared her shoulders, determined not to give him more reasons to exploit his magnetic effect on her.

He half-sat-half-leaned on the massive desk, facing her. He slipped his hands into his pockets, and stared at her for several seconds without speaking. If he intended to rattle her, it wasn't working. Okay, maybe a little.

"Why are you staring at me?"

"I can't figure you out," he said.

"What do you mean?"

He didn't respond immediately. Instead, he twisted sideways and picked something the size of a mini TV remote or recorder.

"This. I've been holding on to it the past three days." He pressed a button.

"It has to look like accident."

Her voice!

Her jaw dropped, and for the first time since he'd accused her of plotting murder, fear coursed through her veins. Was someone trying to frame her for Majid's death? It seemed impossible, but this recording proved someone must have been watching her for at least a couple months now.

"Wh—where did you get that?"

"I guess that answers the question of whether it's you."

Her throat suddenly felt as if saliva hadn't passed through it in days.

"It is, but it's not about your brother."

"Who is it about?"

"I can't tell you."

"Not good enough, India." He ran a hand over his low-cut hair, appearing more frustrated than angry. "Have you committed a crime? Because if you have, I need to know."

"Why? So you can feel free to add your charges to my alleged crimes?"

"So I can offer you protection."

"Protection? That's what we're calling it?"

"Calling what?"

"My imprisonment."

His brows edged up. "You're my wife. It's my duty to protect you."

"Your wife?" Anger resurfaced. She didn't know which part enraged her more. The reference to her as his wife as if it meant something, or the presumption that she needed protection; his, to be precise. "You held a different position the other night."

Surprise jolted through her with the realisation that she'd raised the topic against every promise she'd made to herself every day since.

He appeared unruffled by her comment. He'd probably put it—put *her*—out of his mind the moment he'd walked out of the room. She, on the other hand, had dwelt on it, taken it to her dreams where the vibrator had been foreplay, a foretaste of his own delectable invasion.

He cocked his head, an elusive smile playing around the corners of his lips, making her question the scientifically proven fact that minds couldn't be read. His laser gaze seemed to strip off her garments, leaving her in a mental state of nakedness, and her body heated.

"It would be best not to discuss our private matters in the office," he said.

His high-road response fuelled her rage.

"Private matters? You were prepared to march me in front of the throng of your guests and gratify yourself with my humiliation. What's changed?"

A beat passed.

"I apologise for my actions. I let my emotions get the better of me. I promise it won't happen again."

She blinked, certain she hadn't heard right. His gaze didn't waver, though, and the sincerity in his eyes robbed her of a curt response.

"Can we please discuss the recording?"

Just then, the intercom buzzed, and Moses announced General Khaya. Her heart pounded. Was he about to arrest her? For real, this time? *Oh, God.* Her hands began to tremble. She clutched her thighs to calm the tremors. She should have called Zareb when she'd had the chance.

The door opened, admitting the imposing man who'd met them at Omar's hideaway home.

"I asked General Khaya to be part of this," Omar said. "I trust him with my life. You can, too, but you have to tell us everything."

She contemplated her options. She didn't have many. There had still been no update, which alluded to the possibility that their mission had been compromised. The crank call came to mind. She'd dismissed it, but what if it hadn't been a harmless call? Had anyone found out who she was? She had to trust someone, and despite his occasional harshness and his tendency to think the worst of her, Omar appeared to be on her side.

Her shoulders slumped with resignation. "Sophia Chanda."

He frowned. "Who is she?"

"A former winner of the Most Beautiful Woman in Africa pageant," she answered. "She's also a friend. We attended university together."

"Go on."

"She hated the limelight, so after her reign, she retreated from the spotlight. She continues to work with various charities but shuns media attention. Two years ago, she married a man called Paul Da Silva."

His eyes widened. "The Angolan businessman?"

She nodded. "He used to be a boxer, so she's no match for him."

"What are you saying?"

"He beats her," she answered. "He abuses her, verbally and sexually."

He swore.

"She told me she's required medical attention on several occasions, but he has a doctor on call, so she gets treated at home." She paused, hoping he would say something. When he didn't, she had to continue. "I hadn't spoken to her since she got married, but we reconnected eighteen months ago when I visited Angola to conduct reconnaissance for venues for the Children's Foundation Ball. She's a patron of their National Arts and Culture Programme, but other than that, she keeps a low profile."

"For obvious reasons," Omar replied. "From what I've heard, Paul Da Silva is a dangerous man. If he has criminal dealings, then he's the kind of man who would do anything to keep his crimes hidden, including murder." He looked straight at her, shaking his head. "And you want to steal his wife from him."

She inhaled deeply, but it didn't do anything to calm her racing heart. "If she stays, he's going to kill her."

"Do you know what he could do to you if he ever found out?"

She swallowed. "That's why we planned to make him think she was involved in an accident. If he thought she'd died, then he'd have no reason to look for her."

"What has been your success rate so far with these rescues?"

"Good." She tried to keep a straight face. "However, we've only done ten since we started two years ago, all successful."

She shifted in her seat.

His eyes narrowed. "What are you not telling me?"

"This is the first time we're taking such extreme measures."

She bit on her lower lip, waiting for him to expound on the senselessness of her actions. Her brothers would. Maybe not in those words, but all four of them were so protective, they were worse than mother hens. To his credit, he didn't deride her, for which she was grateful.

"General Khaya, how much do you know about Paul Da Silva?"

"He's a former world heavyweight champion, went into business after retiring from boxing," the general replied. "He's a big player in the real estate industry, but he's into many other ventures. He speaks prominently against the government but, despite speculations, he has made no moves to actively enter into politics."

Omar shook his head. "No. A political position would draw attention to his business dealings and his personal life. If he has something to hide, he'd rather operate from the background."

"He's believed to be into arms and drugs trafficking, maybe more, but there has never been enough evidence to pin him to anything," General Khaya continued. "He also well-loved for his philanthropy. He puts a lot of money into funding development projects and providing scholarships to underprivileged youths to gain access to higher education."

Good deeds to cover the multitude of his sins. Her friend's words eighteen months ago echoed in her head.

"You happen to know all of this off the top of your head?" she said.

"I make it a point to know something about the world's most influential people, My Lady."

"Every crooked business man is greedy," Omar said. "Before we start faking accidents, we're going to go the diplomatic route."

"Diplomatic route?"

It sounded like a bad idea.

He nodded. "We find something he wants bad enough to trade his wife for."

"I'll get on it, Sire," General Khaya said.

With a salute, he left the room. Her attention returned to Omar.

"Why are you helping me?" She ought to just be happy about it, but she needed to know if she'd done the right thing by trusting him with Sophia's life. "You said yourself, this is a dangerous mission."

"Men like Da Silva give the rest of us a bad name," he said.

She snorted, shaking her head. "By all means, make it about you."

Her eyes widened as she realised she'd spoken out loud. Despite the sarcasm dripping from her words, he smiled. A chuckle followed. She blinked. Why did it sound so strange? Then, it hit her.

"This is only the second or third time I've heard you laugh."

Although the corners of his lips were still slightly curled up, the smile had retreated from his eyes. "I haven't had much reason to laugh lately."

A few seconds elapsed.

"You must miss him."

He didn't respond immediately. Instead, he walked over to a window and gazed outside.

"We had our differences, but he was the best big brother a guy could ask for."

His voice was raw, pained. Out of nowhere, she yearned to comfort him. She rose from the seat and crossed the distance between them. When she reached his side, she placed a hand on his lower arm. He shot a glance at her, looking a bit surprised.

"I'm sorry," she said.

His only response was a nod before he returned his gaze to the distance.

"You never answered my question," he said.

"Which one?"

"Do you need time to mourn?"

She sucked in a breath and released it slowly. She'd thought her avoidance tactics during their previous conversation about Majid had worked. Evidently not. His uncompromising look told her she couldn't wiggle out of this again. Majid's passing had left a mark for dying when she'd survived. That would never change, but she didn't need time—not in the way he meant.

How did she admit it to him, or tell him she couldn't stop thinking about him the way a woman thought about a man? Did that make her heartless?

CHAPTER ELEVEN

Omar watched conflicting emotions play out in her eyes as he waited for a response. Was it wrong of him to push for one? Why did it matter, anyway? She was his wife, after all. Eventually, she'd accept it and cleave to him.

She was your brother's wife first, the needling voice he thought he'd squashed echoed in his head. The thought took root, however, and refused to let go.

Majid would have made a great husband. He'd always been the perfect son, the perfect prince, save for one indiscretion in his teens involving the daughter of one of the palace staff. Having learnt his lesson from that experience, his brother had been on the straight and narrow ever since. No doubt he'd have been an exemplary husband.

Omar, on the other hand, had relished causing mayhem and doing the unexpected. As the spare heir, he'd had more freedom than his brother, and he hadn't wasted it. After all, how could he have succeeded in being the perfect son when his brother already excelled at it?

They were near opposites, he and Majid, their tastes differing in almost everything—cars, hobbies, women...

India was different, though. Majid hadn't chosen her. Even if she was exactly the type of woman his brother might have picked—royal birth, proper upbringing, smart and beautiful. Majid was a stickler to the rules, yet, he'd broken protocol so he and India could ride together to their honeymoon.

Had his brother fallen for her the same way Omar had from the moment he'd lain eyes on her? Dare he hope his brother hadn't managed to snag her heart in the little time he'd had the opportunity?

Ya'Allah, he must be the worst of brothers. Majid's body had barely hit the grave, and here he was hoping India hadn't fallen for him. He'd probably rot in Hell for it, but he didn't withdraw his question. He needed to know where he stood with her.

"I don't know if there's a right answer to your question," she finally said.

He released the breath he'd been holding, though he stopped short of reading into her response. It could mean any number of things. He didn't need hope setting him up for a fall.

"Maybe it's unfair of me to ask."

Not to mention inappropriate. A decent brother would give due reverence to his older brother before touching the wife he'd inherited. However, he didn't have the luxury of time—especially if Uncle Latif intended to make a play for the throne and India.

At the same time, he needed to do it right, because making the wrong move could mean being married to India but never winning her heart; an eventuality that would be much worse than losing her to his uncle.

"You *are* being unfair, but not for asking that," she said.

He raised his brows, curiosity awakened.

"You claim to believe I didn't have anything to do with the accident, and yet, you doubt me at every turn."

He faced her fully, and for several seconds, he stared as he took her in. Her hair had been concealed under a *duku*—a scarf—tied in an elaborate style traditional to many West African nations. It showed off her lovely heart-shaped face, the black velvet fabric making her already expressive mocha eyes sparkle. Widows were expected to wear black so as not to invite undue attention while in mourning; a pointless endeavour where India was concerned, because black made her caramel complexion glow and brought out the brown of her eyes.

Even loose-fitting outfits like the one she wore right now, an ankle-length caftan made of a lightweight, dull-finished fabric, draped over her body in the most alluring way, alluding to the curves underneath. Picturing her lush body put his mind in overdrive until all he wanted was to peel off her clothes and gaze at the beauty they hid—a situation infinitely worsened after the night of the banquet.

Luckily, he had the presence of mind to snap back to the present before he lost himself in her gaze. However, he wasn't fast enough to fashion a response before she continued.

"You seem to operate on the premise of guilty until proven innocent. If you truly believe me—"

"I do."

"Then show it!" She raised her arms, joining her wrists. "If not, then make your accusation official. Put me in cuffs and lock me up, so everyone will know what this arrangement really is."

His mind got stuck on one word.

"Cuffs?"

He raised his brows. His idea of putting her in handcuffs had nothing to do with imprisonment and everything to do with pleasure. An image of her as she'd lain in their bed the other night poured into his mind. Only this time, her hands were tied to the bed's head posts while she writhed beneath him as he savoured the delights of her body.

The stirring in his groin should have been a warning to redirect his thoughts, but he made the mistake of looking into her eyes again, and he was trapped. Under her ensnaring brown gaze, his mental faculties malfunctioned, making it impossible to shut down the deluge of thoughts.

Her eyes widened. With a sense of gratification, he noted the faint hue of a blush touching her cheeks.

Ya'Allah. He needed to learn how to control his desires in front of her. Hadn't he learned his lesson? He cleared his throat as he finally managed to rip his gaze from hers.

"Let's hope it doesn't come to that."

She blinked and shook her head, as if she, too, had been caught in the same trap. He couldn't help the thrill he experienced at the idea of his feelings being reciprocated.

"I should go," she said, but didn't move for several seconds.

Panic struck in the recesses of his brain as he realised he didn't want her to leave or maintain the erroneous assumption that he wasn't on her side. He caught her arm just as she stepped back.

"Don't go," he said, mentally re-arranging his schedule. "Spend the day with me."

"Don't you have a kingdom to run?" she asked, even though her eyes sparkled.

Did she know how sexy she sounded when her voice grew thick and breathy? Could it be a tell-tale sign that she had similar thoughts as he?

"I'm sure the country will survive an afternoon without me," he replied and took her momentary hesitation as a sign of impending victory. "The real question is, are you going to allow us to spend time as just a man and a woman?"

A few seconds elapsed. "Are you asking me out on a date?"

A joyous sensation expanded within him. "There will be food involved at some point, but no, it's not a date."

He still intended to get a kiss at the end of it, but he wouldn't divulge this aspect of his plan.

"I want you to meet someone special to me."

"I need to call home," she said. "I'd already promised to call this afternoon, but after that, I'm all yours."

"I'll pick you up in an hour?"

She nodded, and he finally released her.

"Wear something you don't mind getting a little dirt on and bring a change of clothes."

She frowned. "Where are we going?"

"It's a surprise."

Her eyes lit with intrigue. So, his queen liked surprises. He'd have to remember that. His gaze zeroed in on the gentle sway of her hips as she turned and walked towards the door until she was out of sight. Alone again, he returned to his desk and buzzed Moses.

"Clear my afternoon, and call Madam Ofae," he instructed. "Tell her I'm bringing a guest."

With that taken care of, he mused on his conversation with India. Even though he'd tasked General Khaya with the job of uncovering something Paul Da Silva was willing to barter for his wife, there was always the risk of coming out empty-handed.

India's brazen plan of staging an accident was brilliant in principle. However, there was only one person in the world he'd trust with such a task. He picked up his private mobile phone and dialled.

"Your Royal Highness," came the response after just one ring.

"You've never used a title when speaking to me before, Shaka."

"You we're only a prince before. Now, you're going to be king. Credit where credit's due."

He shook his head. "I have a job for you."

Shaka Dubane called himself a private investigator, but his skills were more specialised than that. With a military background, Shaka had been involved special ops for the African Union Armed Forces. P.I. didn't begin to cover it.

"What do you need?"

He gave a gist of the situation and his proposed plans of action limiting the extent of India's involvement to the fact that she was Sophia Chanda's good friend.

"I'm taking care of the first part here, but if my plan fails, he will know his wife wants out." He paused briefly before ending. "That would put her in more danger than she already is, so I need a fool-proof extraction strategy to get her out if it comes to it."

"Give me forty-eight hours."

"Done."

With that settled, they spent the next five minutes catching up before disconnecting.

Having taken care of that, he sat back contemplating the task ahead of him as king of Sudar. He had plans to transform the kingdom's economy, and one of the main ways to do this was through strategic alliances such as the one with Bagumi, which gave them access to larger markets for their goods and access to certain amenities there were not available in Sudar.

The other route was to open their borders to the world. Even with heavy investment by the monarchy, the kingdom couldn't move forward significantly without opening its borders. The question was how to do this without losing the core of their cultural identity? Once he could answer this question to the satisfaction of the masses, the battle would be as good as won.

***

India arrived at her office, her skin still tingling from overexposure to Omar. His effect on her kept getting stronger by the day, and a part of her questioned her decision to spend an entire afternoon with him. However, the more rational side of her knew his invitation presented the perfect opportunity to find out more about him. In particular, whether his legitimacy was in question and how that affected the treaty between Sudar and Bagumi. She'd give him the courtesy of hearing him out before deciding on her next move—something he hadn't accorded her.

Settling in her executive chair, she pushed those thoughts out of her mind as she focused on other matters. She'd planned on speaking with her family this afternoon, but since she was now going to spend the day with Omar, she decided to call them now. She dialled her brother Zik's number and waited as the phone rang until eventually going to voicemail. Undeterred, she disconnected and dialled again. After getting the same result two more times, she called Zawadi, the oldest of her siblings and the Crown Prince of Bagumi.

"India," he said when he picked up. "I was wondering when you'd finally call me."

"The last time I called, you weren't available."

"You called home, and you know unless it's family dinner night you won't get all of us. Now, you're calling me directly as you should have done already." He had a laugh in his voice, its familiar sound making her smile.

"Is everything okay? Are you getting on well in your new home?"

"Yes," came the automatic response.

"Good."

A moment of silence ensued. She released a heavy breath as an urge to confide in her brother gripped her. Having been betrothed since the age of ten, he'd never had the luxury of allowing himself to fall in love or choose a spouse. This made him one of a handful of people in the world who could empathise with her.

"How is your fiancée doing?"

"She is well."

"Do you think you could grow to love her? If she hadn't already been chosen for you, would she be your choice?"

"Those are unproductive thoughts, sister. I've never questioned my obligation to marry her. That's what matters."

"You make it sound like a business transaction."

"That's what it is. The kingdom comes first, you know that," Zawadi said. "If love grows from it, that would be a bonus, but I'd be wise not to hold my breath."

She sighed. She didn't know why she'd even asked, since her own marriage was essentially a transaction. She'd approached it objectively when she'd agreed to marry Majid, but now that fate had thrust Omar into the mix, she found herself wanting more.

She recalled the apology he'd given, how he'd limited it to the night of the banquet. Did he not feel sorry about anything else? Why did she have this crazy yearning for something more when he clearly had them pegged as just a contract?

"I don't know if my marriage will offer Bagumi or Sudar what it hopes for."

"What's going on, India?"

"Omar and King Rafael believe I could be involved in the accident."

There. She'd said it. Let the chips fall where they may.

"Are you?"

She gasped. "No. Of course not! How could you even ask me such a thing?"

"Have you been arrested or formally charged?"

"No." She frowned as his composed tone occurred to her. "Why don't you sound shocked or outraged?"

Her brother kept things close to his heart, so she supposed even if her news had shaken him, he'd still deal with it in his usual calm fashion. Notwithstanding, she'd expected a little more alarm in his tone. Then again, until Omar formally charged or arrested her, what could Zawadi or anyone else do?

"I already know."

Surprise shook her. "You do? How?"

"How else? He told me everything?"

"Why would he do that?"

"Because he's a diplomat, and he won't risk mine or our father's wrath by levelling such an accusation without giving us the chance to prepare a defence." He paused. "Also, I think he cares about you."

She snorted. "He has a funny way of showing it."

"What do you mean?" She heard the alarm in his voice. "Has he been…improper with you?"

"Improper?" She rolled her eyes. "Could you be any more *kolo*?"

"Old-fashioned or not, you need to tell me if he's been—"

"No." Unless three night ago was considered improper. "Of course not."

Her brother was sweet and caring and acted way too old for his age.

"Would you confide in me if he has?"

Clearly, she needed to end the conversation before it got weirder.

"I'd be on the next flight to Bagumi," she replied, and then changed the subject. "I promised to call everyone this afternoon, but something's come up, so please tell them I'll call tomorrow instead."

"Okay, but you better call Mama Sapphire now. I heard her complain that you've called everyone but her."

She laughed. Her mother could be full of drama sometimes. They'd spoken since she'd arrived at the palace, but it had been a video call with her and Queen Zulekha, and of course, her mother wanted undivided attention from her younger daughter.

"Noted."

They said their goodbyes, and she hung up. Next, she called her mother and spent the next ten minutes listening to arrangements for Isha's wedding and her sister's general disinterest in the details, much to their mother's displeasure. Having got that done, she checked her time, realised she had another twenty minutes to spare.

She booted her laptop and opened a browser in incognito mode. Relief flooded her when she found a message from Marianne. Their latest rescue had finally gone through without a hitch. The woman and her five-year-old daughter already had new identities and a safe place to stay. Employment would be arranged for her soon.

She went on to check her regular email for updates on the Children's Foundation Gala. She found only one new email, and it was from the organising team. Her heart plummeted when she read the subject line: *Bad news.*

Events were always like that. One crisis after another. A successful event was really the ability of the organisers to manage the issues and avoid any serious catastrophe. Despite psyching herself, chords of worry curled up her belly and limbs as she read the content of the email. They had lost their conference venue. With only a few months to go, this came as a blow, and that wasn't even the worst of it.

The ministry in charge of tourism, arts, and culture in Angola had retracted their patronage due to the withdrawal of funding for their National Arts and Culture Programme. Sophia's organisation! Her heart began to pound. This couldn't be a coincidence. Somehow, she knew Paul Da Silva had something to do with this. Cutting Sophia off from the event meant taking away any legitimate opportunity for her and her friend to communicate without drawing undue attention. Had he somehow found out about their plan? Was Sophia safe?

She stared at her phone, every instinct urging her to call her friend. Caution stopped her. If Paul Da Silva suspected anything, the call could make things worse and put Sophia in more danger. Still, she couldn't sit idly by. She needed to talk to Omar. Perhaps she could convince him to buy into her original plan.

She shut down and packed the machine and cable in its bag and stood. Just then, a knock sounded on the door.

"Come in."

The door opened, and Salma entered.

"Good, you're back. You're better now?"

"Yes, My Lady."

"My plans for this afternoon have changed, so you can take the rest of the day off. Maybe spend time with your sister?"

Salma smiled, although she looked a little surprised. "If you're sure, My Lady."

"I am."

After dismissing Salma, she headed for the residence to change as she recalled Omar's final instruction on their outing. She'd have the perfect opportunity of discussing Sophia while they were away.

Although worry still coiled around her insides, because of her friend's predicament, the thought of spending time with Omar had her heart beating with unexpected exuberance. She found herself looking forward to the not-date.

CHAPTER TWELVE

Omar noticed the worry on India's face the moment he saw her.

"What's wrong?"

Her eyes widened slightly. "How can you tell something's wrong?"

"I notice many things about you. Spending time with you is an everyday lesson in all things India." It sounded cheesy even to his own hearing, but it was the truth. "Tell me in the car."

He expected her to protest, but to his surprise, she nodded.

The driver was waiting when they stepped out. With the car door already open, Omar assisted her to sit before going around to the other side.

They moved out, sandwiched between two security vehicles.

"Do you believe the safest place in the car is behind the driver?" India asked.

"There's no real research supporting that, but my brother believed it." They'd had more than enough intellectual arguments on that and other topics. "Why do you ask?"

"You've made me sit behind the driver each time we've ridden together," she replied. "Majid also said so when he insisted I move to the driver's side."

He frowned. Something about what she'd said sounded an alarm, although he couldn't immediately tell what. He mused over it for a few moments and eventually pushed it to the back burner. He'd revisit it later. Right now, he needed to find out what had put anxiety in her eyes. He raised the privacy glass.

She watched it until it had rolled up completely, then she looked at him.

"Now, are you going to tell me what's wrong, or will you continue to beat about the bush?"

She swallowed. "I think Sophia could be in danger."

He kept a straight face. "Have you spoken to her?"

She shook her head. "I got an email. There's a problem with the funding for her organisation. They can't put up the show. Without the Arts and Culture Programme, the ministry has pulled its support. I think Paul Da Silva may have something to do with it."

He'd wanted to wait and hear back from Shaka before mentioning anything to her, but seeing her worry made him change his mind. He didn't want her taking matters into her own hands and putting both her and Sophia in danger.

"I spoke with a friend of mine after you left my office," he started and gave her a summary of his conversation with Shaka. "I'll tell him your concerns. If your friend is in danger, I'll give him the green light to extract her. We'll worry about Da Silva later."

"Do you trust him?"

He nodded. "Explicitly. If anyone can do it, he can."

"Okay."

Her other predicament presented a solution for his own dilemma.

"About the venue, why don't you have the gala here in M'Bamina?" he said.

"Really?"

"The exposure would be good for Sudar." He launched into his pitch. "I did my research. The gala attracts some very influential people across the globe. It will be the ideal opportunity to showcase our kingdom to the world. We'll host it at the Palace. The ballroom is bigger than your venue for last year."

Finally, a smile broke forth, and the worry in her eyes receded. "It sounds perfect. After the tragedy Sudar has faced, a party would bring positive media attention, and that's bound to boost the general morale."

"Exactly."

"If you want to showcase Sudar, then we can make it a weekend or even full-week affair. We can set up palace tours, meetings with potential investors, a royal concert…there's so much we can do to showcase Sudar."

Perfect was right. This could be exactly what he needed to subtly soften his people's hearts to the idea of opening Sudar to the world.

"I'll tell my team about it as soon as I get a chance," she said. "Thank you, Omar."

"No, *ya amira*, thank you."

Having settled that, she sat back, admiring passing scenery. The grasslands of the Sudari countryside had become lush four weeks into the country's rainy season. Interspersed with trees, mostly acacias, it presented a picturesque scene. While she looked outside, his interest remained on her. She'd maintained the velvet *duku* but changed into black denims and a dark grey, three-quarter sleeve cotton shirt. The dark colours were perfect for the task they had ahead of them.

A herd of gazelle in the distance caught her attention. She chuckled at a calf skipping around as if aware of her admiration. Her show of excitement brought on a smile. He liked seeing her like this.

She turned suddenly and caught him staring. The smile on her lips faltered while her eyes softened and the soft spot at the base of her neck throbbed. A cloak of warmth enveloped him.

"You love animals," he said.

"I do."

"You didn't bring a pet with you. Do you have any back home?"

She shook her head. "I like dogs, but my father's allergic. I've always thought I'd get one or two when I have a family."

She blinked as if she hadn't meant to say those words. His mind latched on to the word family. She'd thought about having one; perhaps not specifically with him, but he intended to change that.

They continued to converse for the next forty minutes until they entered a fenced compound through the open wrought iron gates of Madame Ofae's Pottery Farm. The car slowed to a stop in front of the main cabin, a five-bedroom unit that served as a guest house. Seven other huts completed the kraal style set up serving as a pottery school and a retreat.

As they got out of the car, a middle-aged woman exited and approached them.

"Omar," she said, opening her arms.

He leaned forward, embracing her. "How have you been, *Eima*?"

He called her aunt, even though they weren't related.

"Getting old."

He laughed. "You don't look a day older than when you left Sultan's Palace."

The woman gave him a swat and a girlish giggle that made her appear far younger than her sixty-five years. Her laugh hadn't changed through the years.

"*Eima*, meet India." He turned to her. "India, this is Madame Ofae, my governess until I turned thirteen, the official age I was deemed to be too old for a nanny and grown enough for a man servant."

She extended her hand, but Madame Ofae pulled her into a hug. Not expecting it, India stiffened briefly before relaxing. Madame Ofae had that effect on people, which was why he hadn't been able to let her go after her service with the royal family had ended many years ago.

After they parted, Madame Ofae motioned ahead. "Come in."

They followed her inside. She left the door open, creating privacy by drawing the curtain. The living room had been converted into a formal reception area and souvenir shop. The rustic, lived-in feel with stone floors and hand-crafted furniture hadn't changed over the years.

India swept a wide gaze, taking in the local art and various ceramic, porcelain and earthenware crafts on display in glass cabinets.

"In addition to selling the most beautiful ceramic ware in the land, Madame Ofae's Pottery Farm lets customers create and paint their own pieces," he explained.

"Some people also volunteer their time to make pieces for my shop, and those are the ones some customers want," Madam Ofae added. "They like the sense of community from buying something made out of love."

"You mean some of these were made by volunteers?"

Madame Ofae pointed at a set of four soup bowls. "These were done by His Royal Highness."

India shot him a glance. "Really?"

By way of reply, he waved. "Pottery and painting relaxes me."

The look that came to her eyes made him want to grab a guitar and create a song just for her, even though he hadn't written as much as a single stanza of a poem in his life. He hadn't even played a guitar in ages. Perhaps the time had come to resume.

"What would you like to do today?" Madame Ofae asked, reeling him back. "Mould or paint?"

"I'll let India decide."

"I've never done pottery or painting." She paused for a few seconds. "I'd like to try creating my own mug. I've always been intrigued by the potter's wheel."

Good choice. If she hadn't done it before, then she'd need a lesson. The thought brought on images of sitting close to her, fingers intertwined. The happy feeling that began when she'd first agreed to spend the afternoon with him intensified. He intended to make the most of it.

***

"Do you live here alone?" India asked as Madame Ofae led them to an outer area at the back where seven huts stood.

"My husband has gone to the neighbouring village for some supplies," the older woman replied. "There's a staff of volunteers who help with our pottery and painting classes. I gave them the afternoon off after receiving Omar's message."

They entered one of the huts. Just like the main cabin, it had a rustic feel, characterised by a stone floor and furnishing that appeared to be handmade.

"I've set up this room for you. The painting rooms are in the main house, in case you wish to try that at some point."

A ripple of excitement coursed through her when her gaze settled on the potter's wheel and a bowl of water in the middle of the circular room. Next to them stood a pan covered with cloth. She assumed it was the clay.

"Thank you, *Eima*, we can take it from here."

"I'll be inside if you need me."

After Madame Ofae left, Omar strolled to a bench to the right where two folded garments lay. "We'll need to wear these."

He unfolded them to reveal double-sided aprons. He put one on and offered to help with hers. She could have done it herself, but for some inexplicable reason, she liked the idea of him helping her out.

"It won't fit over your *duku*."

Without a second thought, she undid the headgear, letting her shoulder-length braids fall unrestrained. She folded the head scarf and placed it on the bench. Her body tingled with delicious sensations as he eased the garment over her head and fastened the side belts. Their eyes met briefly, and a shiver ran up her spine.

His gaze drifted to the potter's wheel. "How do you want to do this?"

"How long does it typically take you to create something like a tea mug or soup bowl?"

"Five to ten minutes."

"Can I watch you make something first?"

With a nod, he took a seat at the wheel. She grabbed the second stool and sat on the other side, facing him. Uncovering the clay, he scooped a fistful and slapped it onto the flat surface of the wheel, then activated it. With full concentration, he began to work the clay, shaping it with deft fingers, occasionally dipping his hands in the water and moulding.

She noted his relaxed look. "You enjoy doing this."

"Yes," he answered. "Doing things with my hands in general helps me to free my mind."

Why did he need to free his mind today, she wondered as she continued to watch his hands. He had long fingers that seemed firm and gentle at the same time. She remembered their feel on her back when they'd kissed. She shook off the thought and refocused on his actions.

She frowned at the current shape of the clay. He'd worked it into an elongated form with a rounded top. *A penis?* She stifled a gasp, her face heating up. He couldn't be making what she was thinking. God, why was she even thinking about penises? He was obviously making a mushroom ornament. Or something. Still, her curiosity got the better of her.

She blinked, getting her mind out of X-rated territory. "What are you making?"

He dipped two fingers at the top, creating a dent. "A candle stand."

"Oh!"

He shot her a glance, curiosity etched on his features. He must have caught the inflection in her voice that suggested a certain amount of guilt.

"What did you think I was making?"

"Nothing."

The corners of his lips curled up as if he knew exactly where her mind had been. *Oh, God.* She needed to work on masking her thoughts better.

To avoid going down that path, she nodded at him. "Can I ask you a question?"

"You can ask me anything, *ya amira*, and you can ask anything of me."

She nearly smiled. His oddities were growing on her.

"Is succession to the throne of Sudar in dispute?"

He frowned. "What makes you think it is?"

"Sheikh Latif said something at the party," she replied. "I got the feeling he didn't like you taking over."

"He doesn't," he said in a matter-of-fact tone.

"But he's your uncle. Family should stick together, no matter what," she said. "That's what my father always taught us. The royal house must hold itself to a higher standard."

"In our chequered history, brother has risen against brother, son against father," he said. "In case you haven't noticed, my country is steeped in many dated customs."

She gave a snort of laughter. The practice of wife inheritance was certainly as dated as a custom could get.

"The purists are determined to restore even those we've managed to change," he continued.

"Purists?"

"Those who think I'm being radical with my plan of opening up our borders to foreign businesses and the international community. They fear the dilution of our culture, and for some, I'm the embodiment of the slow deterioration of our culture."

"Is it true you wouldn't have been eligible a few years ago?"

He stopped the wheel and looked at her. A pained look flashed in his eyes, telling her what she needed to know.

"There was a time one needed to be of full Sudari parentage to become king."

"Yes, I read about that, but how does it affect you?"

"Queen Shaida, my biological mother, was from Northern Ghana."

She noted how he referred to his biological mother by name and Queen Azmera as *a'ma*—mother.

"Was she not of royal birth?"

He nodded. "She was, but when the rule was in force, that wouldn't have mattered."

While he moved the newly completed candle stand to a sideboard, she processed the new information. Like the other day when she'd learned about the male-preference succession, her fight-or-flight instinct kicked in. Could she really be queen of Sudar? Would she be loved or hated when they found out she wasn't going to be just another pretty face happy to simply smile and wave?

"Is Sudar ready for change?"

"Whether it's ready or not, it needs it." He faced her, looking sexier than any man sporting an apron and muddy hands had the right to be. "I suppose your next question would be whether I'm the one to bring that change?"

He paused for a second. "I wasn't Sudar's first choice, but circumstances brought me here, and I won't shirk my duty even if certain factions, encouraged by people like Uncle Latif, don't like me or my ideas."

"I'd like to hear more about your ideas."

"You will, but right now, you're going to learn how to make pottery." He returned to the wheel. "Come closer."

She swallowed. The thought of being in close quarters with Omar made her heart race. She pulled up her stool and settled next to his.

Instead of sitting side-by-side, he moved his seat and settled himself behind her. His musky scent invaded her sense. Despite the heat suffusing her entire back as his nearness, a shiver ran up her spine.

He dipped sideways and scooped some clay, then bringing his arms around her, he placed it on the wheel.

"What shall we make, *ya jameel*?"

He spoke in her ear, the deep tone sending another shiver up her spine. *Love,* her mind provided as an answer. No matter how fascinating the idea of creating something with him, it was his gentle touch and tone that had her heart thumping and her body humming.

"Anything."

Was that husky voice hers?

"You need to centre the clay," he said, taking her hands and placing it on either side of the clay. "It helps to achieve an even thickness of the piece you're creating."

"Ok."

He started the wheel.

For the next few minutes, they worked together moulding her clay, him telling her what to do while his hands guided hers. Her entire body began to tingle as her skin continued to heat up from the points where they touched. If she didn't do something about it, she'd slowly combust.

"How did you get into pottery?" she asked.

"*Eima* used to have a day off every week when she worked for us. I kept pestering her about what she did with her time off. That's how I got the moniker Royal Pain."

Imagining him as a persistent little boy made her smile and proved to be exactly what she needed to get her mind off how good his arms around her felt.

"When she finally told me about her love of pottery, I immediately started reading up on it." His voice echoed with unmistakable affection. "I think next to my mother, I loved her the most. When they said I no longer needed a nanny, I didn't want to lose *Eima,* so I enrolled in her class, which forced my parents to send me here every week."

"They didn't mind?"

His soft laugh vibrated through her, sneaking into hidden corners of her being.

"They were ecstatic I'd found a distraction that kept me out of trouble," he said. "Once I started, though, I discovered it helped me to clear my mind."

They fell silent as she realised she had no more questions, nothing to distract her from his nearness, his heat. Focusing on their intertwining fingers, she realised a bowl had emerged from the clay.

"All done," he said. "Not bad for a first try."

She scrutinised the finished product. "It's a little crooked, but it's the cutest bowl I've ever seen."

He produced a wire and coached her through the process of running it under the bowl until it came loose. When he stood, she immediately missed his heat. Carefully, he lifted the bowl off the wheel and placed it next to the candle stick on the sideboard.

"Now, we leave it to dry a bit. *Eima* will do the hard work off trimming."

She chuckled, lifting her clay-covered hands. "I thought the hard part is what we just did."

"No, we did the dirty work."

She laughed. This playful side of him was unexpected yet refreshing, and it made him so damned tempting. In an unanticipated gesture, he tapped her nose with his forefinger, smearing some clay on her. She gasped, and without thinking, she did the same to him.

An awkward moment followed, and they stared at each other. Next thing she knew, he'd palmed her face, covering her left cheek with clay. She hadn't had time to dodge. Without warning, laughter erupted from her. As she attempted to pay him back in kind, he ducked and instead caught her around the waist.

She screamed, attempting to wriggle out of his grasp, but it was too late. He easily finished the job he'd started. The tussle continued until she found herself wrapped in his arms, facing him, their lips only inches apart.

He looked a sight with his Nubian nose smudged with clay, but she must have looked worse with almost her entire face covered in mud. Her laughter faded as tension charged in. She expected him to kiss her, but he stilled, as if waiting for her next move. Some invisible force propelled her to lean closer. She raised her hands again and cupped his cheeks, inadvertently painting his face, too. If he minded, he didn't show it. In any case, her mood was far from jovial.

Being in his arms, feeling his breath on her face, felt good. With sudden clarity, she realised she had every right to enjoy closeness with him, to touch him, to desire him. Her heart expanded. She *liked* Omar, loved having his strong arms around her. For the first time since waking up in that hospital bed, guilt didn't wrap around her at the thought. She wanted Omar, and that was okay.

She rose on her toes, touching her lips to his in a tentative kiss. He still didn't move save for his lips responding to her. Emboldened, she licked his lower lip, savoured it with light nibbles.

He grunted, his arms tightening around her, pulling her to himself. Something solid pressed into her abdomen, revealing his desire. A moan rose from her. She pressed further into him, wanting to feel more of him as the kiss intensified. After a moment, she pulled back to stare into his eyes. He smiled, heat emanating from his gaze.

"Perhaps I erred in not bringing you here earlier," he said, his voice husky, and it went straight to her centre.

Something vibrated between them before the ringtone of a phone filled the space.

He took out his cell phone and checked the screen. "It's Faridah. I'll call her later."

"No, take it," she said. "It could be important."

As he answered the call, she attempted to pulled out of his arms and allow him to speak. However, he held her firm, his fingers lightly caressing her back. The contact stimulated her already heightened senses, making her want to snatch away the phone so they could pick up where they left off.

"What is it?" he said to Faridah.

Although she could hear Faridah's voice, she couldn't make out what she was saying.

"Okay, I'm on my way."

He didn't speak for several seconds after he'd clicked off.

"Is something the matter?"

He looked at her. "I guess I was wrong. The kingdom couldn't survive an afternoon without me."

CHAPTER THIRTEEN

Omar bit back a curse. What the hell did Uncle Latif want now? Faridah hadn't wanted to talk over the phone, but he guessed it couldn't be anything good.

"What's happening?"

India's voice reeled him back. He looked at her. She hadn't freed herself from his arms; proof he hadn't imagined it. She'd kissed him. Did it mean something, or had she simply acted in the heat of the moment?

"We need to head back," he said. "The Royal Council is requesting for an emergency session, and my father has called it."

"Why?"

"I don't know." He inhaled deeply, pushing his own questions aside. "Unfortunately, lunch will have to wait, but I'm sure Madame Ofae can whip up some sandwiches for us. I hope you don't mind."

"Of course not."

After cleaning up the place, he led India to a guest chalet normally reserved for him. While she showered, he found Madame Ofae in the main building. Before he could ask for the sandwiches, she offered to make them *shawarmas* with some freshly baked flat bread from her kitchen.

"You're a gem, *Eima*. Thank you."

She waved a hand, though her delight showed on her face. "Anything for you, my prince."

He took his time returning to the chalet, and when he got there India had finished washing and changed into a flowing boubou similar to what she'd been wearing prior to their trip.

He proceeded to the bathroom. As the cool water pelted his skin, his mind drifted back to a few minutes ago when she'd been in his arms, kissing him. Disappointment lodged in his chest as he imagined how the afternoon could have gone, especially following that kiss.

There'll be more afternoons.

With that thought as his reassurance, he finished up and got dressed.

When they returned to the main building, Madame Ofae met them holding a paper bag with the wraps. Since he had water and other drinks in the car, he didn't impose further by asking for more. After extracting a promise from him to return the following week and paint their crafts, she enveloped him in one of her motherly embraces.

"It will be well," she said.

No, she wasn't clairvoyant, but he still appreciated her words of encouragement.

"Thank you, *Eima*."

After releasing him, she hugged India, as well. "Take care of him."

India nodded as though she understood exactly what Madam Ofae meant. That made one of them. Besides, he didn't need taking care of.

Madam Ofae stood and waved as they departed. Settling back, his mind drifted to their previous conversation about the safest seat. He still hadn't figured out why her comment had sounded off. Something about Majid insisting she move to the driver's side. It came back haunting him, yet remaining tantalisingly out of his reach.

"India, why did my brother ask you to move to the driver's side? Why didn't he seat you there in the first place?"

She looked at him askance. "The driver had already seated me before Majid came."

"Wait. Are you saying he joined you and not the other way around?"

How the hell had he missed that?

"Yes, he sent away his convoy and joined mine."

"But it was his driver at the wheel."

"We swapped drivers. What difference does it make?"

"The tire was tampered with," he explained.

"We already know that."

"On your car." A chill ran up his spine as the words made it to the open. "The accident couldn't have been meant for Majid. It was meant for you."

She stared at him, disbelief etched in her expression. Even he had trouble wrapping his mind around it, but the truth couldn't be denied. Somebody wanted India dead.

***

For several seconds, she sat frozen until her thoughts converged on one word. *You.*

"Me?"

"Whoever tampered with the tires couldn't have known Majid would break protocol."

Her heart raced while her head continued to spin. A few seconds elapsed, and then…she laughed, because this had to be a joke. Right? Any second now, he'd tell her it was a cruel prank and render an apology.

He didn't. Instead, he took her hand, forcing reality to pierce through her denial.

"Who would want to kill me?"

"I can think of at least one person," he replied, concern knitted through his brows.

Her right hand flew to her mouth as the only possibility occurred. "Paul Da Silva?"

"Somehow, he must have found out what you were planning. In which case, you may be right about Sophia."

She shook her head, though it did nothing to assuage her disbelief as she went through her mind. *Where did I slip up?* She needed to warn Marianne. If Paul Da Silva knew about India, then he certainly knew about Marianne.

Omar whipped out his phone. The rest of the journey, he was on the phone barking out instructions.

An hour later when they arrived at the palace, she still reeled from the news, which had unleashed the fear coursing through her veins. Five ominous words kept echoing in her head.

It was meant for you.

Omar got out of the car and opened the door for her. The moment she stepped out, they were surrounded by half a dozen guards. Was she in danger even at the palace?

As if he'd read her mind, he gave a small smile. "It's just a precaution."

Two of the guards retreated when they entered the building.

A delegation of three men led by Uncle Latif and a stern-looking woman met them. They were all middle-aged, the women wearing a formal boubou and the men dressed in similar traditional attires. She recognised the woman as one of Omar's aunts.

"Uncle Latif," he said. "*Eima* Alima."

"I'm not here as your aunt," the woman responded.

"Then what is it?"

"We're calling for an emergency meeting of the Royal Council," she replied.

India noted the stiffness in Omar's stance. She hadn't known him long, and yet, she recognised the gesture. He was pissed.

"You have no right or basis to call for a Council meeting."

"No, we don't, but your father does," Uncle Latif said with confidence that denoted truth.

"We have become privy to information regarding the accident that took your brother away from us," his aunt explained. "Information we believe you should know."

"It involves Princess India," one of the other members said.

Anger flared in her. If she wasn't still reeling from the truth—which these people obviously had no idea about—she'd have defied all social graces and hit the woman across the face. She didn't miss their accusatory looks aimed her way. Condemned in their eyes without a trial. They needed someone to blame, but their eagerness blinded them.

Omar's drawn lips and the angry flare of his nose gave her the assurance that he was on her side. As the woman stepped forward, he raised his hand.

"Lay a finger on the would-be queen of Sudar, and you'll lose the entire hand!"

His aunt froze, as did the others. Except Sheikh Latif. He appeared unperturbed. In fact, he seemed to be enjoying the unfolding scene as though it was going exactly as he wanted it. Was this his doing?

She returned her attention to Omar, noticed the flexing of his jaw muscles. Had she been at the receiving end of his rage right now, she might have cowered. She thought she'd seen him angry at her, but that had been nothing compared to this. Her own anger appeared like mere annoyance against the fury in his voice. Eyes narrowed, jaws tightened, and hands balled into fists, he looked like a predator about to make mincemeat of his prey. His aunt's eyes widened.

She shouldn't feel gratification at that, and yet, she couldn't help the satisfaction swelling within her.

"Lead the way. We shall have this emergency session you've instigated, and you'll discover the imprudence of your actions." He turned to her, and all the anger vanished from his face. "Come, *ya amira*."

Crazy. She was crazy. Why did she feel glee at this partnership with Omar? It was more than that, though. She cared about him, cared what happened to him and what he thought about her. The fact that he stood in her defence against his people told her everything she needed to know, and it went straight to her heart.

Head held high, she followed him. They approached large double doors flanked by two guards. A third man stood in front of the door. General Khaya. He held a folder in one hand. As they reached him, he bowed to Omar and then to her before handing over the folder to Omar.

"Everything you asked for, Sire."

Her heart raced, a spark of hope lit within her. Curiosity lured her into a desire to ask about the contents, but reason stopped her. There hadn't been enough time between now and when Omar had called him in the car with the new information. Whatever lay in the folder, it couldn't have anything to do with whoever wanted her dead.

One of the guards opened the door, and they entered what she assumed to be the Royal Council chamber, an austere-looking room with a throne at the far end mounted on three steps. Twelve ottomans, six on each side, flanked the path to the throne, where she supposed the members of the Royal Council sat for meetings. King Rafael sat on the throne but rose as she and Omar met him.

"I didn't have a choice, Omar," he said.

"I understand, Baba." His voice was low, the response meant only for his father, but she was close enough to hear. "I know you want answers, too."

"Do you have them?"

"I do."

King Rafael's attention moved to the Council members filing in. "As I have already relinquished active duties, Omar will preside over this meeting."

She didn't check for their reaction, but she imagined they wouldn't be too pleased with the king's edict.

Omar took her hand and led her to the first seat on the right side of the throne. She sank gratefully onto it. The king now sat on the seat opposite hers while Omar took his place on the throne. Despite his casual attire, he didn't look out of place on the seat of ultimate power. It suited him.

"Don't bother sitting," he said to the members as they approached the ottomans. "This won't take long."

An uneasy chill seemed to grip them as they exchanged worried glances. She reckoned this wasn't going the way they'd envisaged.

"Sheikha Alima, would you care to expound on the information you claim to have?"

"They are text messages which appear to implicate Princess India."

"In what way?"

Sheikha Alima's gaze didn't waver, but India saw hesitation in her demeanour. "I have not seen the exact wording of the text messages."

"And yet, you felt unwisely confident to call for a meeting." He didn't bother masking his contempt. Opening the folder in his hands, he read out the transcripts. "Does that about cover the extent of this new information you've become privy to?"

"There is a tape," Sheikh Latif started.

"This one?" He produced the recorder and played the tape from her conversation with Sophia. Another exchange of glances followed.

Sheikh Latif wasn't smiling anymore, though he still didn't appear as uncomfortable as the others.

"You had all this evidence, and you were sitting on it?" one of the others whose name she didn't know spoke for the first time.

Omar pinned him with his gaze. "Evidence? Since when is it Sudar's style to besmirch a person's good name with unsubstantiated material?"

More uncomfortable stares. She'd have laughed if she weren't still smarting from their arrogance and the slur cast on her character as though she were some common criminal. Even then, would she not be entitled to a fair hearing?

"Though it hasn't been made public, it's clearly no secret among us that the accident wasn't an act of nature. Someone tampered with the car's tires," he continued.

"Your Royal Highness, we agree the evidence isn't much, but isn't it enough to probe further into their meaning?" another member asked.

"I've spoken with Princess India, and I'm satisfied with her explanation of the context of these conversations. Her innocence in this matter isn't up for debate."

"Omar..." his aunt began.

"I'm not presiding here as your nephew," he cut in. "You shall not address me informally, Sheikha. Neither will you interrupt me."

Sheikha Alima's eyes widened, her face drawing into a stiff mask. India nearly felt sorry for the older woman.

"Now let me give my bit of new information. You missed one vital piece of the puzzle," he continued. "Majid dismissed his convoy and joined India's. Whoever tampered with the car couldn't have known of my brother's plans."

Even though she'd had at least an hour to digest this news, a shiver ran down her spine. She'd had a brush with death and that had chilled her to the bone, but knowing someone had actually planned it for her, that the person was probably still plotting to fix the mistake, numbed her.

Perhaps she'd been too sheltered, had grown up surrounded by too much love that she couldn't fathom why anyone would commit such a heinous crime. Yet, she'd helped enough abuse victims to know the hate and evil residing in some people's hearts. People like Paul Da Silva.

"Who, from Sudar, would want Princess India dead?" another member asked.

"Why are you assuming it's someone from Sudar?" someone else countered.

"Why would somebody from another country decide to commit such an act on a foreign land?"

"Perhaps they saw a weakness in our security or leadership," Sheikh Latif said.

Silence followed. All eyes went from him to Omar. It hadn't escaped anyone's attention that the Emir of Umm Jafar had cast a challenge to his nephew. Had it eluded the older man that Omar hadn't been at the helm of affairs when the accident happened? Did it even matter to him?

Omar didn't take the bait. His anger seemed to have died down, although his entire body language made her think of a wild animal that had been caged, waiting to pounce.

"We don't know why anyone wants India dead. We made a mistake assuming Majid had been the target, which means we may have been looking in the wrong places," he said. "Now that we've been steered in the right direction, I intend to weed out whoever it is, and when I do, God help them."

A few seconds elapsed before he continued. "When I have real news, I'll inform the Council, but until then, I hope you'll believe I want justice served as much as you do."

He finally had them on his side, she deduced from the nods of assent.

"Needless to say, the new information must not leave this room. We don't want to lose any element of surprise we may have." He got another murmur of general acceptance. "If there's nothing else—"

"There *is* one thing," Uncle Latif said. "Since the members are here, should we not discuss your coronation?"

"What about it?"

"You haven't set a date, Your Royal Highness," Uncle Latif said. "I take it you are unable to, seeing as your bride still wears her mourning clothes."

She blinked. *What?*

"I guess the rumours are untrue, then? You don't have the ability to charm the clothes off every woman."

She stifled a gasp, unable to believe the message her ears had transmitted to her brain. Her face heated up from the blood simmering underneath the surface.

"Do you have a point, Sheikh Latif?"

"I have only the best of intentions. Sudar needs a substantive king, and since you clearly haven't fulfilled the most basic requirements of your marriage—"

"He has."

The words came out without warning, but she kept a straight face, daring anyone to question her.

Sheikh Latif didn't appear to be fazed.

"My Lady—" he said in a tone which sounded conciliatory, although she couldn't help picturing Kaa, the snake from *The Jungle Book.*

"The next words out of your mouth better be an apology to Princess India," Omar warned.

His uncle bowed, appearing to take the hint, although the unabashed upturn of his lips suggested otherwise. "I'm sorry if I spoke out of turn. Please accept my apologies, Princess India."

Twelve pairs of eyes watched her. A beat passed as she composed her voice.

"No," she said.

A collective gasp went around the room. Even Sheikh Latif had his brows arched up in surprise.

She stood.

"In Bagumi, my word is incontestable, my honour without blemish, but the moment I married into your royal family, I've been treated with nothing but disregard and disrespect by the people who should have been prepared to defend my name without question."

Once she started, all the pent-up anger seemed to fuel more words.

"I was passed on from one son to the other without the courtesy of my consent, accused by you without a fair hearing, my good name sullied by your words, and you think 'I'm sorry' covers the multitude of your sins?" She now stood in the middle of the assembly, casting her gaze around the room, pausing on each member. "I know your hearts are broken, and the truth about the accident doesn't change the fact that Prince Majid died, but you don't get the right to question, doubt, or imprison me."

She looked at Sheikh Latif.

"Why am I still in mourning clothing? Because my imprisonment precludes me from fulfilling the basic right of a widow to say goodbye to her dead husband. So, no, Sheikh Latif. I don't accept your apology, and I shall wear black until the day I see fit."

"Surely—"

"Enough, Sheikh!" Omar snapped, sweeping up from his seat. In a few strides, he stood head to head with his uncle. "You should accept when you're defeated."

His uncle straightened his posture, a crease in his brows indicating his displeasure.

"I'm not defeated, Nephew. As we speak, the necessary rites are being performed to enable us to approach the Sacred Stone." He glanced at her. "We'll see, then, who's defeated."

CHAPTER FOURTEEN

The little vein on top of his right eye began to twitch. It wasn't visible, he knew, but he also understood what it meant. He was this close to losing it with his uncle. He sucked in a breath, reminding himself that violence didn't solve problems. It would teach his uncle a valuable lesson, though. Luckily for the older man, Omar would rather talk than fight any day.

"This meeting is over," he said.

The Council members came to bow before him before filing out, leaving his father and India. The outgoing king rose from his seat and walked over to India. Omar couldn't help noticing the slight slouch in his father's posture due to a spinal condition. The doctor had recommended a walking stick. He'd soon be unable to walk without one, but for now, the old man insisted on defying the doctor's orders.

"India, Sudar owes you an apology," his father said. "*I* owe you an apology. Omar asked me to trust him, but I'm a grieving father impatient for answers. I allowed my brother to take advantage of my moment of weakness."

Omar let out a breath. He could only imagine what Uncle Latif had said to goad his father into calling a Council meeting. The rivalry between the two men had often been one-sided, with his father always prepared to see the best in Uncle Latif and the latter taking undue advantage. He thought by now, his father would know better, but perhaps there was truth in that saying about blood and water.

"I shall not ask forgiveness for myself, but I hope you won't punish Omar for this," his father continued. "In an ideal world, we'd have waited for you to awaken before taking any action, but time was of the essence, and the alternative would have been far less desirable. You have to know my son acted with honourable intentions."

Honourable intentions. He nearly snorted. His selfish goals outweighed the honourable, but luckily, his father had no clue about the former. He'd keep it that way and hope it didn't come back to haunt him.

He might have spaced out for a few seconds, because he didn't catch her response.

"I'll leave you two to talk," his father said and turned to leave.

The moment the doors shut behind his father, she turned to face him.

"What did he mean?"

Her wary tone suggested she expected the worst of explanations. He didn't like hearing the mistrust in her voice, but he couldn't blame her for it. He could only hope she'd understand after she'd heard him out.

"Baba shouldn't have said anything."

"Nevertheless, he did, and I want to know what he meant by time was of the essence and the alternative being less desirable."

He exhaled heavily. There was no longer a reason to keep the details away from her. In truth, he should have told her the moment she'd woken up from her coma. He'd convinced himself it was for the greater good, but his heart knew the truth. He'd been afraid of making his case worse and losing her altogether. Would today confirm those fears or prove them to be unfounded?

"When a woman marries, she becomes part of her husband's family. If the husband dies, it's his family's duty to secure the future and well-being of the widow and her children. That's the intention of wife inheritance."

"Except I'm not poor and without means of taking care of myself."

The sarcasm in her voice put an uncomfortable kick in his pulse, but he plodded on. "Understandably, not every brother wants to marry his once sister-in-law, so there's flexibility in the law."

Her eyes narrowed. "Meaning what?"

He was much bigger, taller, and stronger than she, yet, anxiety crept into him.

"It isn't the sole right of the immediate next of kin. Any eligible kinsman can step up. In the case of the Crown Prince, anyone with a claim to the throne could have stepped in. I had to act before someone else did."

"Someone else?" she replied, and her eyes widened with understanding. "Sheikh Latif?"

"Marrying you would have forced the Council to bypass the normal line of succession to make him king instead of me."

"Due to the alliance," she said.

He nodded.

"You married me to secure your place on the throne."

Her words cut him, yet, he couldn't deny them. He still needed her to understand.

"It was about more than the throne." Why the hell was his heart beating so fast? "I couldn't live in a world where you belonged to him."

A moment of tense silence ensued, his words hanging between them like an elephant in the room.

"He still means to challenge me for the throne."

Worry sneaked into her eyes. "Can he?"

"Unfortunately, our laws allow it under extenuating circumstances, which this happens to be." He shifted as discomfort tightened around his chest. "If there's a dispute or any reason why the expected presumptive heir is deemed unfit, then succession can only be confirmed by consultation with the Sacred Stone."

She blinked. "The what?"

"The Sacred Stone," he repeated. "Legend has it that it fell to Earth from the Heavens many centuries ago."

He told her about the Great War of Succession and the sorcerer, Amon, who summoned the Sacred Stone, knowing this story might just seal Sudar's fate in her mind as the most backward nation in the world.

Whatever she thought, she hid it well. Her expression remained unreadable as she listened with an unwavering gaze and without interruption until he was done.

"If the Sacred Stone is so powerful, won't it know you'll be a better leader?"

A soft laugh broke out of him. "Thanks for the vote of confidence, but it doesn't work with human rationale. Its primary purpose is to preserve the royal lineage. Uncle Latif may not be a nice guy, but he's of royal blood, has full Sudari parentage, and he already has heirs, which I don't."

"Unless you—" She stopped. "I mean, we…"

"Yes," he answered her unspoken question.

Silence ensued as her brown gaze ensnared him. His mind immediately shifted from the sacred stone and succession matters to her—only her. Those bewitching eyes of hers did that to him. Her succulent lips made him crave for much more than her warm kisses.

He pushed those thoughts aside. This was neither the time nor place to allow his libido to take control of his brain. Besides, he wanted more than her body; he wanted her heart.

"We need to shut down your uncle," she said.

"We?" He stepped towards her, bringing the space between them to barely a foot. "Does that mean you've decided to remain my queen?"

"I don't think I have a choice in the matter."

"You do." *Ya'Allah.* What was he saying? If he were gambling man, he'd be on the verge of losing it all. "You can end our marriage on the grounds that I haven't fulfilled my marital rights to you."

There. He'd given her an out. Time to transmit the message to his brain. He needed to stop fantasising about a future with India. Pain jabbed him in the chest at the prospect. He wouldn't dwell on it. He could survive losing her, as long as he didn't think about it.

There were, after all, more pressing issues at hand. He needed to focus on her needs and desires. One, in particular, would surely snuff out any sexual urges and fantasies.

"When would you like to visit Majid's grave?"

***

India blinked. It took a few seconds for his words to register. Disappointment lodged in her belly, pushing against the thrill his stare and proximity had roused. Words eluded her.

"For what it's worth, I was going to take you there. I just thought you needed time," he continued. "Under the current circumstances, I think you should limit your exposure until we're sure your life is no longer in danger."

She forced the corners of her lips up in a futile attempt to pick herself up. "Of course."

Her response forced its way out of strained vocal chords. What was wrong with her? How could she be thinking about his lips and his touch when she should be more concerned about her safety? Her mind had stopped functioning when he'd stepped towards her. She'd expected—*no*, she'd wanted—him to kiss her. Instead, he'd told her she could walk away. Now, all she could think about was the crushing pain in her chest as if her heart was being ripped out.

"What is it, India?"

"I thought you wanted to—" She blinked, recovering from her momentary distraction. She couldn't let him see what his words had done to her. If he wanted a divorce, she'd give it to him. She had too much pride to beg for a marriage she'd previously spoken against. "It's nothing. I should get going."

She turned to leave.

"Stop." His voice was low, but the command was evident.

Her legs froze while her heart thumped.

"You thought I wanted to what?"

"Kiss me."

She grimaced. How pathetic was she? Nothing that had happened in the past nearly two or three hours warranted her intense desire for Omar right now. *Get a grip, girl.* She needed to get out before she made a fool of herself.

The sound of his soft footsteps rooted her to ground. He stopped behind her, radiating heat into her body even though he hadn't touched her. His hand slipped around her waist as he brought her flush against his body. She sucked in a breath at the unmistakable rigid shaft digging into her back.

"Do you feel that?" he whispered in her ear.

Pleasure shimmered in her abdomen, and her body trembled as her breathing hiked. God, why did his touch have to feel so good, so safe, even after he'd spoken of divorce?

"Answer me, India."

She nodded.

"Then you should know I'm in a constant state of arousal whenever I'm around you. I ache for you, *ya amira*," he said. "I don't want to just kiss you. I want to touch between your legs and feel you get wet for me. I want to strip off your clothes and spread you out before me."

His lips grazed her neck, setting her body on fire.

"I want to taste your wetness, *ya jameel*, and pleasure you with my tongue until I have you panting and begging for my possession."

His thick voice brought his words alive, forming images in her mind. Her nipples tightened in response, and her own desire had turned into a wet, throbbing ache. His hand slipped underneath her shirt, singeing her flesh. She moaned.

"I want to bury myself deep inside your heat and make you forget anyone else who's ever touched you, *ya qalbi*." His hand rose to her breast, tweaking her highly sensitised nipple, and her knees nearly buckled. "I want to feel your body tremble, hear your cries of gratification when I pour my seed into you."

Suddenly, he withdrew his hand, robbing her of the delectable sensation of his touch. She wanted to whimper and beg him to continue.

He released her completely. "I can't do any of it unless you ask."

She whipped round. Their gazes caught.

"Are you asking, *ya rouhi?*"

She nodded.

"Not good enough."

He stood so close, he could easily bend forward and join their lips, but his posture remained ramrod straight, his hands pocketed. He appeared unruffled; yet, she saw beyond the façade. His dilated eyes and measured inhalations betrayed him. She knew, however, he wouldn't act on his desire unless she said the words.

"Are you asking, India?" he repeated.

"I'm asking."

Her voice was low, yet, it sounded loud in her ears. Several charged seconds went by, and neither of them moved. Had he heard her? Would he kiss her already?

Finally, he released a breath and took a step forward, taking her hand. "Let's go."

***

They took the long route through the gardens separating the work areas from the residences. Omar had chosen this in a deliberate attempt to enable his body to calm itself. It might be the more scenic route, but he could only think of the woman walking beside him, the woman his heart desired. It took every ounce of restraint he had to keep from hoisting her over his shoulder like a caveman and rushing her to the residence.

He felt her stare and turned. She gave him a little smile before her gaze faltered. God help him, or he might just give in to his primal instincts, after all. Ten excruciating minutes filled with stolen glances and secret smiles took them from the Royal Council chamber to their private quarters. He dismissed the bodyguards and unlocked the door, holding it open for her to enter.

The moment they were inside, he pulled her into an embrace. She leaned against him, draping her arms around his shoulders. Her eyes sparkled.

"Say it again, *ya amira*," he said. "Let me be sure I didn't imagine what you said."

"Kiss me, Omar. Touch me. Everything you said."

His breath whooshed out. Now he feared he might actually be dreaming. If he were, then he may have to will himself to never wake up and end this scene. He dipped his head and gave her the kiss he'd been yearning for since they'd been interrupted at Madam Ofae's. His desire hadn't abated even with the Royal Council's unwise actions. If anything, they'd roused his protectiveness and magnified his desire for her.

The moment their lips touched, he was done for. Her exquisite tongue mated with his as if they'd been doing this dance for a lifetime. She pressed into him, her softness against his hardness. She was playing with fire; only, he was the one at risk of combustion. He grunted. His eager hands sneaked under her shirt, touching her smooth, warm skin. *So soft.* His heart shuddered.

Without breaking the kiss, he whisked her around, backing her up until he had her against the wall. She grabbed his collar, fumbling with his buttons. Her fingers seared his neck. Her scent intoxicated him. He fought for control as his hand found her right breast, cupped it. *Perfection.* His fingers stroked the hardened peak. She moaned.

He pulled away, staring into her eyes as he continued to fondle her nipple while his other hand began to unbutton her shirt.

She groaned, sucking her lower lip between her teeth and biting on it. She abandoned his shirt and tugged at the waist of his jeans. Her breathing had become erratic, much to his pleasure.

"Patience, *ya jameel*," he whispered, freeing her breasts from the confines of her bra. "Let me have a taste first."

He opened the shirt and took one perfect nipple in his mouth while kneading her other breast. Deep moans sounded from her as her hands cradled his head and her body succumbed to the pleasures of his ministrations. He loved her scent, loved the way she moaned and shivered when he kissed her skin.

Moving from her breast, he trailed his tongue up to her neck, tasting the salty sheen of fresh perspiration. He went farther up, caught her earlobe between his teeth and nibbled. A sharp intake of breath sounded in his ear.

"Are you wet for me, India?" he whispered as he groped at her jeans button and zipper, undoing both without difficulty.

He sipped her lips as his hand slipped into her jeans. Her hips arched up. Her moans rose unrestrained, her breath coming in spurts and gasps. After the night of the banquet, he thought he'd seen her in heat, knew what to expect. The other night had been the tip of the iceberg. It hadn't prepared him for her passionate responses to his touch, the liquid desire in her eyes as she stared into his.

He palmed the V between her legs, feeling her wetness on the tip of his fingers. She whimpered, rising on tiptoes and thrusting her hip forward.

"Do you ache for my touch, *ya amira*?"

"Yes, Omar," she whispered.

With a satisfied moan, he slid his hand farther down, parting her feminine folds and touching her slick, swollen bud. Her body trembled. He stroked and circled. She cried out his name in a moan of pleasure, rocking her hips in rhythm with his gentle strokes.

"*'Ant alqamar walnujum*," he mumbled. "You're the moon and stars."

Tonight, he would make her his, even as he was already hers. From the first moment he'd set eyes on her, she'd snagged his heart. Her first kiss had ruined him for any other woman. Now, she purred in his arms and called out his name, branding him further as if her possession of him wasn't already complete.

She licked her lips. "I ache for you."

Ya'Allah. If she kept that up, he wouldn't be able to stretch this out, but if he took her now, he wouldn't last.

He kissed her, burying her moans in his mouth. With his free hand, he pulled down her jeans so he could touch her more intimately. He slipped his finger into her slick heat, felt her body clench around his digit. She sagged against him, sucking on his tongue. He hooked his finger and twisted his hand until he found the spot that made her cry out, her body squirming and jerking.

"India, *ya omri*," he murmured.

He couldn't wait to be inside her, to be one with her, to feel her inner muscles spasm around his shaft as it did around his digit.

She bathed his face in kisses as he felt her approach the peak.

"Omar," she moaned.

With his next stroke, he pushed her over the edge, held her while she twisted and contorted, digging her nails into his skin as her climax swept her. He continued to stroke her until the current of her release brought her back.

He pulled out, brought his hand to his nose, and inhaled her intoxicating scent before sucking her intimate juices. Her liquid brown eyes widened, her lips parting. In spite of her release, desire poured into her eyes more intense than before. She pressed against him, and his erection jerked. He gave her a long, lingering kiss before pulling back again.

Habibi, ya nour el ein. She was the light of his eye.

Yearning still burned in her gaze.

"What is it, *habibti*?"

"I want more," she said. "Make love to me, Omar."

He'd wanted to stretch it out, give her at least one more release before taking his pleasure. The plea in her voice and her eyes unravelled his plan. He'd give her what she wanted, everything she wanted.

"Have you ever been tied before?" he asked.

CHAPTER FIFTEEN

India's eyes widened. "Tied?"

She knew about sex play, of course, but she hadn't tried it before. Even the vibrator as a wedding present had scandalised her—although that may have been due to opening it in front of her mother and some of her aunts at the bridal shower. As far as she was concerned, bondage was a level up.

She swallowed, meeting his gaze. "You're into kinky sex?"

Her voice didn't sound nearly as shocked as she'd expected.

"Not in the extreme." His lips curved in one of those sexy smiles, and liquid warmth curled in her belly. "Aren't you?"

She shook her head.

"Your sex toy is purely for self-application, then?"

Her face heated even though delectable sensations continued to swirl in her lower abdomen. She wasn't used to this kind of conversation even during foreplay. However, his casual tone and the way his hands petted her face and neck felt natural, stirring her desire.

"I haven't—" she amended her statement. "Hadn't used one before."

He frowned. "Why do you have it, then?"

"A wedding gift from my sister. She slipped it into my suitcase without my knowledge."

He raised his brows, intrigue lighting up in his eyes. "I assumed you were just trying to get out of—"

She didn't let him finish. "I wasn't."

"I acted irrationally out of frustration. I apologise." He leaned forward and placed a peck on her lips. "Or am I also undeserving of your forgiveness?"

"You've redeemed yourself since."

"Good."

He pulled back and rid her of her denims, then without warning, he swept her into his arms. A scream erupted from her, which segued into giggles. She held on to him, gazing into his eyes as he transported her from the living room to the intimacy of their bedroom.

"We'll eventually mark territory in every room, but for the first time, we shall put our stamp here in our room and on our bed."

He set her to her feet. She kept her hands around his neck, unwilling to part from him.

"Your eyes," he said. "They tell me you want something."

"I've never seen you naked."

His brows shot up as if he hadn't expected it. *Good.* She could also be full of surprises.

"*Mafish mushkila,*" he said. "Undress me."

His heated look added a kick to her heartbeat. *Calm down.* She reached for his shirt, forcing herself to unbutton it at a steady pace, rather than just ripping it open as she wanted to. She peeled it off his shoulders, and he shrugged, letting it fall to the floor. Her hungry gaze roved over his bare torso, pausing on a scar across the left side of his chest. She touched it lightly.

"A reminder to never attempt to break up a bar fight," he explained.

Her heart lurched. "Did it hurt?"

"It did."

She leaned in and kissed it, wishing she could erase the memory of the pain he'd endured. She kissed every inch of it before she eventually licked his nipple. He groaned. She enjoyed the feel of his smooth skin underneath her palms for a few seconds before resuming her task of undressing him.

She reached for his trousers, unbuckling the belt and unfastening the button on top. Then, she unzipped him and pushed down the trousers. He helped by taking it off.

She stared at his erect manhood, currently stretching the limits of his briefs. Her gaze met his as she placed her palm on it. He was rock hard and warm even through the fabric. She wanted to hold him.

"Take it off, *ya jameel*."

Her hands shook slightly as she hooked her thumbs through the waistline and pushed it down, releasing his erection. Her sharp intake of breath made her heart race faster. She swallowed. She wanted him inside her. Now.

He would, she reminded herself. Eventually.

"Touch me," he said.

Her hands closed around his shaft. He seemed to swell further in her hands. Her hand moved across his length to the base and then to his tip, rubbing pre-cum oozing out. He sucked in a breath.

"You see what you do to me?"

His voice sounded laboured. She smiled, her hand movement gaining audacity. He groaned, briefly shutting his eyes, then his hand closed around hers, stopping her.

"I'm at breaking point already. What you're doing is bliss, but it's also torture."

"Is that why you want to tie me up?"

"Only your hands. If they are on me, I won't last even five minutes."

The rush of excitement came as a surprise. Was she really considering letting him tie her? There was no denying it, though. She liked knowing she held that power over him, that she wasn't the only one losing control.

"If you don't want to be tied, then you must promise to keep your hands to yourself."

She took in the magnificent body before her while she continued to rub him. "I don't make promises I can't keep."

"Then we're going to need a scarf," he stated. "Where do you keep your *dukus*?"

"Great. I'm getting bound with my own scarf." She couldn't keep the smile off her face.

"I have turbans, but they are too big and not nearly as soft as your silk scarfs."

"Check the drawers."

He led her to the bed and sat her on it.

"Don't go anywhere," he said as he backed away.

She laughed. This was a new side of him: funny and attentive and caring. She inhaled deeply, her body buzzing while she waited. Anticipation thrummed within her. She dropped her gaze to her clothes. Her shirt lay open and off her shoulders. One of her breasts was still fully exposed while the other had somehow slipped halfway back into its cup. Should she fix herself up or undress? The latter, she decided after a moment, and started to take off the shirt.

"What are you doing?" Omar's voice interrupted.

She turned and caught her breath at the sight of him. He was truly stunning—all sculpted dips and planes. How could he appear even more imposing in the nude? Did he know the meaning of vulnerable?

"I'm undressing," she said.

He tut-tutted. "When I said I want to take off your clothes, I meant it literally."

Now, she should be used to the shivers and tingles his voice induced, but it still stole her breath. He came to squat in front of her and took over the task of ridding her of the shirt. With a pleased look, he stared at her bosom. Her eager nipples beaded instantly.

He grunted in approval before stroking the exposed one, sending shards of pleasure down to her centre.

"I love your nipples," he whispered. "They're big and so sensitive, so perfect."

Her intimate muscles quivered. He raised himself and took it in his mouth, gently suckling on it. Desire intensified in her core. He moved to the other breast, nipping the peak with his teeth, then sucked her through the lace of her bra. A sharp jolt of pleasure sent anticipation to the heat between her thighs.

Too soon, he pulled back, raising the scarf.

"Lie down."

"You aren't taking off the bra?"

"No," he replied in a raspy voice. "This excites me more."

To her surprise, she didn't feel self-conscious as she lowered her torso onto the bed.

"Before we start, we're going to need a safe word," he said. "Would you like to pick one?"

She inhaled, letting it out in a slow breath. Was she ready for this? Staring into his soft eyes, she realised she trusted him. She could do this. She wanted to relinquish control of her pleasure to him. He'd already demonstrated his skill in satisfying her desires. Earlier on with the Royal Council, he'd also shown he cared about her.

"How do you say 'stop' in Arabic?"

Her question pleased him, if his smile was anything to go by.

He touched her face. "*Tawaquf.*"

She repeated the word.

"Very good," he said. "Now, place your hands above your head."

Catching his gaze, she did as he asked. His smile reassured her. After he'd secured her wrists, he stretched out beside her.

"It's not too tight. If you jerk hard enough, it might come off," he said. "Your job is to make sure it doesn't."

Her heart raced as, in reflex, she tugged her hands. It appeared secure enough.

"What if it comes undone?"

"Then, I'm going to have to punish you."

Her eyes widened.

"Don't worry, you'll enjoy this punishment."

A thrill zinged through her. She didn't have time to react before his lips descended on hers and stopped any further conversation. He rose over her, his hands sliding up her arms. She kissed him back, rubbing her legs against his, since he hadn't tied them.

Pulling away, he moved down her body, pausing on her breasts. He released her confined breast, brushing kisses around her areola. Her nipples ached for attention. He angled her enough to unclasp the bra, but her tied hands prevented him from taking it off. He pushed it up and lowered his mouth on one nipple, then the other, leaving the first feeling bereft and cold.

Her breath rapidly became sharper, faster. He abandoned her chest area, caressing her stomach, then her waist. When he reached her panties, he planted open-mouthed kisses along her pelvis. She shuddered inside.

An "Ooh" rushed out of her. She'd never known how sensitive she was there. Fire and ice deluged her as he kissed a path to her toes. He spread her legs, then used the tips of his fingers to trace lines from her feet to the apex of her thighs. She whimpered, understanding what he'd meant by bliss and torture. She wanted him to get rid of the panties and touch her again.

"I thought you were at breaking point."

She nearly didn't recognise the hoarse, impatient voice that emanated from her mouth.

"I am, *ya amira*, but I need to get you ready for me."

He pulled the seat of her panties aside and slid two fingers into her.

She moaned. "I am."

"Are you nearly in tears?"

Tears? What she felt was joy and pleasure…need.

"No."

"Then, you're not ready."

She whimpered. He lowered his lips on her pelvis again as his fingers continued their sweet invasion. She writhed beneath him as her need became an ache. Her hands jerked, slackening the restraints a fraction. She held her breath. He didn't appear to notice, but she made a conscious effort to keep her wrist together. However, the effort to stay still intensified the effect of his actions. He did that thing again, hooking his fingers and touching the spot that made her lose all inhibitions.

"I want you." She panted. "I'm ready."

Thankfully, he pulled down her panties and tossed them somewhere at her feet.

"Open your legs, *ya amira*. Let me taste you."

Her heart shuddered. Waves of delight and anticipation washed over her as she did his bidding. Desire intensified in his eyes.

"Do you know how hard it was for me the other night, watching you and not having permission to touch you? To see your wetness and not be able to taste you?" His voice was low and thick with arousal. "Now I know I misread your desire. I'll make up for my mistake."

He caressed her inner thighs, fuelling her impatience. She called out his name, but the rest of her plea became a groan as he parted her folds and lowered his mouth on her.

She cried out, arching up. Her inner muscles spasmed. As she writhed, the scarf loosened a little more. She stilled again, trying to contain the explosion of pleasure and realising she was losing the battle.

"Omar," she cried. "Please…now."

He didn't relent for several moments.

"Omar… Oh, God…"

"Are you nearly in tears, *ya amira*?"

"Yes," she whimpered. "Please…"

He raised his head. The respite did nothing to lessen the full-blown ache in her womanhood. Still kneeling, he leaned forward, lifting her by the waist and settling her around his tip. Her inner muscles squeezed. Though his bulging muscles told of his strength, she was still mesmerised by his power as he kept her propped up with one hand. He leaned forward, bracing himself on his other hand.

Staring into her eyes, he drove into her in one fell swoop, and her world titled on its axis. She gasped. He stiffened, his body shaking as though he was barely holding on. A deep sound emanated from him. After a moment, he pulled out slowly, letting her feel every thick inch of him. He slammed into her again, stretching her inner muscles beyond what they'd ever experienced.

Each time their bodies met, a shudder forked through her. The feel of him inside her defied words. With cries of gratification, she welcomed his invasion, again and again. This was bliss. It registered in some obscure corner of her mind. God, why had she resisted his touch for so long? Why had she deprived herself of this? She was meant to be here, meant to be with him.

"You feel so good, *rouhi*," he murmured.

He leaned further forward, catching her nipple in his mouth. His name spilled out of her lips. Their groans mingled as he paid homage to each breast, mumbling endearments between kisses.

His rough tone heightened her pleasure. Her mind only registered the feelings of ecstasy he invoked in her. Suddenly, all the sensations began to converge in her womb. Her inner muscles tightened.

"Omar," she cried out again and again.

"*Na'am*, India," he replied each time.

He pumped faster, deeper. She lost control, her body movements becoming frenzied. Her hands suddenly came free. She didn't pause to register it. Instinctively, she reached for him, pulling at him, urging him to go even deeper.

A harsh cry sounded from him. Liquid warmth spilt into her just before she lost all awareness. She became weightless, soared on clouds of rapture. He kept moving, extracting every ounce of release from her until she lay still, her body light and replete.

He stretched out next to her, staring into her eyes as he cradled her in his arms. A cosy sensation washed over her, seeping deep into the recesses of her being.

"You've undone me," he whispered.

She smiled at him, still waiting for her mind to be able to form words. She touched his face and kissed him.

"You freed your hands."

She remembered his earlier promise. "Am I going to be punished, then?"

His lips curled up. "Severely."

Somehow, she knew said punishment, just like him tying her today, would bring her pleasure.

"Habibi, ya nour el ein," he whispered.

Her heart shuddered. "What does that mean?"

"My darling, you're the light of my eye."

She held her breath. How could he make such a declaration? They'd only known each other what? Two months? Even as she thought this, she knew a change had occurred in her heart.

"I've fallen in love with you." His hand covered her cheek. "Is it so hard for you to believe?"

"How can you say so with such certainty?"

Her toes curled with the smile he gave her.

"Do you remember the first time we met, *ya amira*?"

She nodded, thinking back to the day; how a simple handshake had sent a bolt of lightning up her arm.

"I knew my brother's intended would be visiting, but the moment I saw you, I prayed you weren't her." He laid back, staring at the ceiling, although his arm around her continued to rub her. "You were wearing a Ghana-style *kaba*. It had an orange background, with yellow and blue diamonds. It made your skin glow."

She exhaled. "You remember what I wore?"

"I remember every word you spoke, every time you smiled."

The implication of his words stunned her to silence.

"It hit me you weren't mine. I'd have to watch you blossom beside my brother, see your body swell with his heir." A beat passed. "You know what I did the moment

I left my father's office? I got in my car and drove to Madame Ofae's."

"Is that why you didn't join us for dinner?"

"You noticed my absence?"

She nodded.

He returned his gaze to her. "I spent the weekend there trying to get you out of my mind. I made plans to resettle outside Sudar after the wedding."

Her heart thudded, stunned anew at his confession. Several seconds elapsed.

"I can't wait to see you in vibrant colours again," he said.

"Would it please you if I wore my normal clothes tomorrow?"

"Very much." His voice sounded strained. "However, I'll be patient while you observe your respects to Majid for however long you decide."

His words pierced her heart. The gruff tone made her realise her words to his uncle had hurt him.

"What I said at the Council meeting wasn't meant for you."

He shook his head. "Don't feel pressured. You're well within your rights to observe the full mourning period."

"Look at me, Omar."

He trained his gaze on her.

"I'll go back to wearing my regular clothes from tomorrow."

"*Habibi, ya nour el ein,*" he whispered again and lowered his head to the crook of her neck, nipping her flesh with his teeth.

Flutters invaded her belly. She sighed and snuggled closer. At that inopportune moment, her stomach growled. She froze.

He pulled back. "Forgive me. I've kept you without food."

She bit her lower lip. A mixture of relief and disappointment lodged itself within her. She was hungry, but she didn't want to leave the warmth of his arms.

"I'll have the kitchen bring us something," he said. "After you're fed, we'll talk about your punishment."

***

Contentment bubbled over in Omar's heart, overflowing into his every pore and crevice. He couldn't remember a time in his life when he'd been this happy. Knowing she'd finally accepted him had his heart beating with exhilaration.

She halted his attempt to get up by tightening her arms around him. He succumbed, engaging her mouth in a slow dance of lips and warm tongues to the music of their soft moans. His delight and desire for more manifested immediately, and he had to force himself to pull back.

"I need to feed you." His voice had grown thick and husky. "After that, *ya rouhi*, you can have me."

She whimpered but released him. He basked in the glow of her sensual stare as he slipped out of the bed and found his trousers where he'd abandoned them. She pouted when he put them on and secured the zipper without bothering with the button. He retrieved his phone, which was still in his back pocket. "Any special requests?"

"Aside from chocolate cake?"

She giggled, and his heart expanded. He'd never tire of hearing her laugh. This open and fun side of her came as a pleasant and most distracting surprise, which he made a mental note to explore later. Since he had Pierre on speed dial, he called the chef directly and placed

India's order along with a request for something that wouldn't take too long to prepare.

After disconnecting the call, he started toward the bed. "Where were we?"

The words had barely left his lips when his ringtone pierced the air. Frowning, he checked the screen and stopped in his tracks.

"I'm sorry, India, but I have to take this." He swiped the screen as he exited the room. "Faruk?"

"I'm sending you something," his cousin said. "It's everything you need to stop my father."

Omar sucked in a breath, relief washing over him. Even though Faruk and Uncle Latif had a difficult relationship, he'd hated involving his cousin in the matter.

"Thank you, cousin," he said. "I'm sorry for putting you in a position to go against your father."

"As a royal of Sudar, my allegiance is to the throne. My father's actions are in direct conflict with my beliefs."

"Still, your loyalty to me will derail any effort you've made to mend your relationship with him. I know that's why you returned to Umm Jafar after all this time."

"Only at my mother's insistence," Faruk answered. "Good luck, Your Royal Highness."

"Thank you, Faruk."

After the call, his phone beeped with a series of notifications. The information Faruk had spoken of had come through.

Disbelief slammed into him as he swiped through evidence of treasonous acts perpetuated by Uncle Latif. He swore. Anger and hurt surged within him. He'd suspected his uncle of some grave crimes, but nothing to the extent of what he held in his hand.

Reeling in his emotions, he made two more calls—one to Moses, instructing him to send invitations for another emergency Royal Council Meeting for tomorrow, and the other to General Khaya to alert him about the evidence he was about to forward for his urgent action.

With those settled, he returned to the bedroom. India sat up immediately, a frown knitting in her brows.

"What's wrong?"

So much for controlling his emotions.

"Everything is right, *ya amira*. I've received information that will stop Uncle Latif for good."

CHAPTER SIXTEEN

Two Royal Council meetings in two days. That had to be a record, but it had been necessary under the circumstances. They'd pestered him about setting a date for his coronation, and now, he would. More than that, he needed to put Uncle Latif in his place. The earlier he got through with the meeting, the sooner he could return home to India. She'd opted to work from the residence this morning, which worked perfectly with his plans.

The moment he wrapped things up here, he'd meet briefly with General Khaya for an update. If he didn't hear from Shaka by then, he'd have to contact him, too, and then, he'd call it a day. Surely, he could get one lovemaking session in before lunch time. They'd skip lunch altogether, if he had his way.

The thought put a healthy kick in his heart rate. He noticed a speck of pink thread on his sleeve and brushed it with care. He'd chosen a wine-coloured dashiki, a good match for the predominantly pink outfit she'd picked out for herself.

He'd never been into matching clothes and all that lovey-dovey stuff, but he'd never been in love before, so he guessed he couldn't say anything with much conviction. The other reason he'd chosen this loose outfit instead of a suit was that it could better hide any physical manifestation of his inability to keep his mind off India.

Yesterday, while waiting for their food to arrive, they'd lain in bed talking and cuddling, two things he'd never done before; yet, no other conversation had meant this much to him. He'd ensured that the meal included snacks for later, since he'd had no intention of letting India out of his sight for the rest of the day.

They'd eaten in their birthday suits, which had led to some interesting foreplay with the whipped cream that had come with the fruit salad. Later on, withholding her climax as penalty for freeing her hands had been punishment for him, as well. It had led to the most intense release of his life. When she'd cried out his name in a deep, guttural moan of satisfaction, he could have died right then, and he wouldn't have cared.

He pushed the thoughts aside, returning his focus to the meeting.

"Now that we have the coronation date settled, we need to decide who will be crowned. Sheikh Latif has made enough insinuations about challenging me."

"Prince Omar, I only want the good of the kingdom. This isn't personal," Uncle Latif said as part of his speech to the Council about why he was better suited for the position of king.

The nods of approval from at least four of them told him his uncle had done his homework lobbying them before a vote had to be called. Thankfully, as acting king, he still presided over the meeting.

"Bribery and corruption," he replied. "You think those bode well for Sudar?"

"I don't know what you're talking about?"

"Don't you? You've been charging extra tax to your people, but the ordinary citizens of Umm Jafar receive no extra benefit for this. Many of your officers are involved in high-level bribery. Cases brought against them mysteriously disappear in your Royal Court.

"My father has always been too trusting of you, given you too much autonomy. As long as the crown received your portion of taxes and no blatant human rights abuses appeared to be happening, he trusted your fabricated reports."

"You ought to be cautious about the words you allow yourself to speak, Your Royal Highness," his uncle said. "These are serious accusations you're voicing against me, a man of royal Sudari blood."

Omar gave a snort of laughter. These weren't new accusations. There'd always been rumours, but his uncle had covered his tracks well. Or so he'd thought.

"I've conducted my own investigation, Sheikh Latif, so believe me when I say you can't wiggle out of this one."

"Taxes can be refunded to the people," one of the members obviously on his uncle's side said.

"Bad seeds in his court can be weeded out," another added. "Surely, his entire court isn't corrupt."

He nodded.

"Unjust taxes shall be refunded or funnelled back into the system. His trusted advisors who are in it with him will face the consequences of their bad judgement. The rest will be rewarded with higher responsibilities, but not before the real problem is dealt with." He looked at his uncle. "I've found that if you cut off the head, the rest of the body usually dies."

"Leadership isn't for the faint-hearted," another said. "Surely, there are reasons for Latif's actions. I've known him for decades. He's an honourable man."

"Then you must be blind, Alhaji Jahma. Sheikh Latif has some good qualities, but honour isn't one of them." He went on. "The role of emir or king is like that of a husband. He safeguards the safety of his family, goes hungry to ensure they are fed, protects them by putting himself between them and any danger they may face. He doesn't loot their coffers to fill his. Any man who cannot sacrifice his needs for his people doesn't deserve to be a leader."

His uncle shifted, beginning to look uncomfortable.

"I would have been happy to forgive his actions if bribery and corruption had been the worst of his crimes."

"What are you talking about?" Sheikha Alima, who'd been unusually quiet during the meeting, asked.

"We finally broke one of the Nassiru brothers who confessed to information we've uncovered." He returned his gaze to his uncle. "Would you like to tell them what I learned, or should I?"

Uncle Latif didn't respond.

"I guess I will. The Sheikh Latif scholarship programme is a front for radicalising young men into subscribing to purist ideologies. Unfortunately, the Nassiru brothers went a step further and thought they'd get rid of the crown altogether." He continued to look at Uncle Latif. "I call that treason."

"Surely, you don't mean that," Uncle Latif said, and for the first time that morning, he no longer carried his usual smug expression. Understandable, since by Sudari laws, the penalty for treason was death.

Perhaps now, his uncle would understand why some of the ancient laws needed changing.

"Is this true, Latif?" His father's voice sounded pained.

He didn't allow his uncle to respond. "The evidence I have is iron-clad, but, by all means, let's hear it from the devil's own mouth."

Uncle Latif had yet to speak in his defence.

"No more words, Sheikh Latif?" He stood and took several steps forward until he stood in the middle of the assembly. "Is there anyone still in support of his claim to the throne?"

As expected, no hand came up.

"I revoke the autonomy accorded Umm Jafar," he said. "Sheikh Latif, you're expected to step down from your seat as Emir."

"Don't do this, Prince Omar," Uncle Latif pleaded.

"Who will he hand over to?" Alhaji Jahma asked.

"Luckily for him, I'm feeling generous. I won't humiliate the rest of his family by removing the emirship from them. His son, Faruk, doesn't subscribe to his father's ideologies, for which reason my cousin hadn't stepped in Umm Jafar for four years," Omar said. "He was instrumental in helping us uncover his father's sins. Do any of you object to this?"

Once again, no hands went up.

"Sheikh Latif, if you don't announce your resignation the moment you return home, The Crown will remove you. Finally, you'll be under house arrest for the foreseeable future." He paused to allow the edict to sink in. "This is me being lenient. Refuse, and you shall be stripped of all your titles and thrown in prison."

After several moments, Uncle Latif nodded.

The meeting ended on that note.

* * *

India stared at her reflection in the full-length mirror in the bedroom. As promised, she'd worn one of her regular outfits. A jumpsuit made from African wax print—tiny green leaves set against a deep pink background, which was softened by white speckles. A bead necklace and earring set, and a pink silk *duku*, finished off the look.

The whole kingdom will know what we did last night.

Her conversation with Omar this morning floated through her mind.

In all fairness, we started well before night, he'd responded, sneaking up behind her and wrapping her in his arms. *You look beautiful.*

He'd kissed and nibbled the junction between her neck and shoulder.

Take it off. He'd turned her around and pressed his arousal into her abdomen. A certain part of me wants to pay homage to your beauty.

She'd laughed. It hadn't taken much convincing after that to get her to undress. The quickie had been just a mind-blowing as last night.

A cosy warmth filled her as memories of their night and morning of passion filled her thoughts. She touched her lips, remembering his kisses.

There was no getting around it. She didn't know how it had happened, but she'd fallen for him. Their lovemaking had been everything he'd promised and more. How was she going to get through today when all she wanted was a replay of everything they'd done last night, all day?

Fortunately—or unfortunately—Omar had left earlier, citing a meeting with the Royal Council. They'd agreed he should put his uncle to shame by setting a date for his coronation. He'd also promised the information he had on his uncle was enough to take him down for good. She was on her own until afternoon, and she'd decided to stay in the residence to work.

A knock sounded at the door. *About time.*

She'd asked Salma to come over, so they could go over her schedule for next week when her official duties would start full-time. If she could convince Omar to let her go out in public. Perhaps she could also use her feminine powers of persuasion. The idea got her heart racing.

She sucked in a breath, focusing her mind on the present. She opened the door to find Salma standing with a cuppa and a box that emitted a mouth-watering aroma of freshly-baked confectionery.

Salma's eyes appeared red-rimmed as though she'd been crying. She did a double-take as her gaze took in India's outfit.

"Is everything okay, Salma?"

The other woman gave what seemed like a forced smile. "You look beautiful, My Lady. This shade of pink becomes you."

Her decision to stay in the residence this morning had been to avoid precisely this kind of reaction. What she did with her husband was no one's business. From now on, it would be that way, so she just had to endure the stares and knowing smiles this once.

"Thank, you Salma. Come in."

She stepped aside.

"Good morning, My Lady," Salma said. "Forgive me for not greeting first."

"It's not a problem. I didn't expect my change in wardrobe to go unnoticed." She pointed ahead, deciding to change the topic. "We can work in the sun room."

A moment later as they entered the sun room, she gestured to an armchair. "Take a seat."

Salma raised her hands. "His Royal Highness asked me to bring you food, since you didn't have breakfast with the rest of the family."

He was so thoughtful and caring. How had she ever thought him to be anything else? Smiling, she took the cup and sipped its contents. It was a herbal brew bursting with flavour.

She moaned. "This is good. What is it?"

"Masala tea," Salma replied. "Sudari red label tea infused with local spices."

She took several sips and explored the content of the box. Alas, none of Chef Pierre's chocolate cake, but the croissants smelled divine.

"If I may be so forward," Salma said. "Prince Omar seems to care a lot about you."

She couldn't help the giddy smile that came to her lips. The mere mention of his name did that.

"I care a lot about him, too." For several seconds, she remembered the look in his eyes when he'd told her she was the light of his eyes. She should have told him she loved him, but she'd been so overwhelmed by his own confession that her voice had failed her. She'd rectify it the very next time she saw him. "Let's start, shall we?"

They looked at meeting requests and filled her calendar. She also had three invitations to speak at events.

"We'll hold all the meetings here at the palace," she said while Salma took notes.

It would minimise the security risk. Omar should be pleased with that. As for the events, he'd have to understand she couldn't hide away in the palace out of fear. It just wasn't her.

After working for about fifteen minutes, an unexpected wave of light-headedness made her pause. She shook her head and blinked. Perhaps she'd exerted more energy with Omar than she'd thought. After all, she hadn't had sex in two years, and even then, none of her previous experiences had been as involving.

"Is everything all right, My Lady?"

She frowned, sitting back. "I feel a little woozy, and suddenly sleepy. Perhaps you should have brought coffee instead."

She drained the contents of the cup, hoping the local herbs had a pick-me-up effect. If they did, the result was slow to manifest. She might have to cut this meeting short and take a nap.

"How did you do it?" Salma asked.

"Do what?" She blinked again, forcing her eyelids open. "Can you get me some water?"

Salma didn't move. "What is it about you that the princes of Sudar can't resist?"

The coldness in the other woman's voice stunned her.

"Salma, what's wrong? What are you talking about?"

"You were supposed to die!" She shot up from her seat.

Everything in her went cold as understanding dawned. "The accident. It was you? Why?"

"He promised her he'd marry her, then you showed up. Beautiful, royalty." She gave a snort. "Instead of manning up, he told her more lies about how your marriage would be in name only. If she gave him a male child first, her son would be king."

The words brought with it panic as it occurred to her how alone they were.

"Your sister? Majid was the man she fell in love with?"

"She was impressionable, and he was literally Prince Charming. He dangled the idea that she could be a princess before her, and she swallowed it all up."

"You know I didn't steal him from your sister, right?"

She had to keep the conversation going, find a way of distracting her so she could get a message to Omar. She tried to move her hand, to reach her phone. Even a simple message like 'SOS' should cause him to at least call. If she didn't pick up, he'd know something was wrong. She hoped.

"She should have learned her lesson when the king sent us packing."

She blinked, trying to keep her eyes open, but whatever poison Salma had given her seemed to be winning the battle. Her hand edged towards the phone. *Just a couple more inches.*

"What are you doing?"

Salma's gaze shot to the phone. India grabbed at it, but she wasn't fast enough. Salma darted forward and shoved the phone off the table. The device disintegrated—body, battery, back cover—on impact with the floor. India stared in horror, her hope for rescue shattered.

Calling up every ounce of energy, she grabbed the box of croissants and tossed it at Salma. She didn't wait to see if they hit her before running for the door.

***

Omar returned to his office feeling like a weight had been lifted off his shoulders. The only thing outstanding was to prove Paul Da Silva had tried to assassinate India, and also rescue his wife, Sophia Chanda. *For India's sake.* He checked his time. *A quarter to ten.* He would have gone to her now if he wasn't expecting General Khaya. Thankfully, the general had been waiting in his office when he arrived.

"Your Royal Highness," he said.

"Good morning, Khaya." His gaze dropped to the folder in the other man's hand. "Any news?"

"Yes, Sire," the general said. "It may be nothing, but you should take a look at this."

He received the folder and opened it. The first thing he saw was the photo of a woman. There was a vague familiarity about her, but it didn't ring any bells. He turned it over. *Nothing.* The next thing in the folder was medical records from Sudar's top mental health facility.

"Nadine Alfadi?"

"Her real name is Nala Khalid."

His eyes widened.

"Nala?" He hadn't heard the name in years. He looked at the photo again. "That's why she appeared familiar."

She was older, and her eyes lacked their youthful lustre, but it was her. Majid's teenage indiscretion.

"I thought they left Sudar."

"They did move to Niger, but it appears the girls lost their mother ten years ago and had to return to distant relatives in Sudar."

"Girls?"

"She had an older half-sister who didn't stay at the palace with them. She lived with her father and his new wife until he passed on. Then, she had to work to supplement her mother's income."

"Okay, so what have Nala and her sister got to do with anything?"

"Look at the visitation log, Sire. It could be nothing, but I wanted to show this to you before taking any action."

He flipped the page and looked at the log. A chill ran up his spine as he read the name of the only visitor, logged consistently on the last weekend of each month for six years.

"*Ya'Allah!*"

The file dropped from his fingers, spilling its contents as he turned and started running.

***

The chair India had been sitting on crashed to the floor. Salma swore. India didn't turn to look, but prayed the chair slowed the other woman down and bought her a couple of vital seconds. If only she could get to the front door. The guards would hear her.

As she reached the living room, Salma's footsteps behind her sounded louder. She made the mistake of looking back, and as she returned her gaze forward, she crashed into an armchair and fell. Her muscles convulsed with pain. Clutching her side, she struggled to catch her breath. She scrambled to get up, but Salma leapt forward and caught her legs.

"You will not get away this time."

"Help!" she screamed.

"No one's going to hear you."

"The guards will."

A cold laugh came from Salma. "There are no guards outside. I sent them away."

"How?"

The guards should not be taking instructions from anyone other than Omar, herself, or the head of palace security. She pulled herself up to a seating position. One leg came free. She kicked. Salma screamed and released her.

As she got up, something collided with the side of her head, shooting a sharp pain through her head. Stars floated in her vision. Though it didn't knock her out, it disoriented her for a few seconds, made her vision swim before her eyes.

Salma was on top of her, holding her hands. As the other woman got off, India tried to move and realised her hands were restrained.

"I'm dating their boss," Salma said, smiling. "How else do you think I got close enough to tamper with your car?"

"You won't get away with this. Omar will find me, and you'll pay for your crime."

Another harsh laugh emanated from her. "He's busy with meetings. He may care about you, but he wants the throne more. Since you obviously spread your legs for him, he's happily planning his coronation. By the time he realises you're not here, you'll be long gone."

Her eyes stung. "What did you put in my tea, Salma? How long is it going to take before I'm dead?"

Salma didn't respond. Instead, she took out a cell phone from her pocket and dialled a number.

After a few seconds, she spoke. "It's done. You need to hurry. I can't carry her deadweight by myself."

Hot tears fell from her eyes. She was going to die without having told Omar she loved him. Her eyelids began to droop. She tried to pry them open, tried to hold on a little longer, though she didn't know the point of fighting the inevitable. She'd drunk all the tea. Whatever poison she'd been fed, she'd taken it all.

A crashing sound jolted her awake.

"What have you done?"

Omar?

She tried to turn, but she couldn't move. Salma spun around and ran.

"Get her," Omar's voice barked.

The next moment, he was beside her, cradling her in his arms. "India."

Joy erupted in her. At least, she got to see him one last time. "Omar, I have to tell you something."

"Don't waste your energy, *habibti*."

"But I lo—"

He wasn't listening.

"Get the medics here. Now!" he yelled. "And find out what the hell Salma gave her."

She grabbed his shirt, forcing him to look at her. *I love you*, she wanted to say, but if she had only one shot at speaking before the inevitable happened, she had to warn him instead.

"Aso—" Her tongue appeared to be falling out of her mouth. She blinked. "A-so-bo."

She managed to get it before everything went black.

CHAPTER SEVENTEEN

"India!"

Omar watched in horror as India's eyes rolled back and her head lolled to the side. His hands shook as he cradled her to his chest. Despite his promises, he hadn't been able to protect her, and now, he was losing her. He checked her wrist and found a slow but steady pulse. She wasn't gone yet. Maybe she could be saved.

Careful to keep her as steady as possible, he lifted her from the floor and laid her on a sofa. He noticed the cable tie on her wrists. The audacity of Salma's actions put anger in him.

"Get me a knife!" he barked at no one and everyone.

Within seconds, one of the guards appeared with a pocket knife. He took it and cut off the restraints, then propped her head up with a throw pillow.

He closed his eyes, offering a silent prayer. He couldn't lose her.

"Where the hell are the medics?"

The image of her lying on the floor with Salma standing over her replayed in his mind. He'd never tasted fear the way he had when he'd entered and realised he'd arrived too late. She'd tried to tell him something. He frowned. *Asobo.*

He handed back the pocket knife.

"Tell them to bring Asobo to me," he said.

The man bowed and headed out. Omar returned his attention to India. He felt her pulse again. *Still there.* But for how long?

"Let me go!"

Salma! At the sound of her voice, everything inside him turned molten. He rose and headed out. He found her in the custody of a guard, struggling to set herself free.

"What did you give her?" he asked. "Does it have an antidote?"

The sweet Salma who'd worked at the palace for six years had disappeared. The woman looking at him now only did so with revulsion. How could she have concealed all this hatred so well for so long? How had *he* never realised Nala had a sister?

She spat at him. Luckily, he wasn't close enough for it to hit its mark.

"Go to Hell!"

"I've never struck a woman before, but I'm prepared to make an exception."

He raised a fist, advancing on her. He repeated his question, his tone menacing. Panic filled her eyes. She shrank back.

"You better start talking, Salma, or this will not end well for you."

"She's not dead," she said in a deadpan voice, as though she no longer cared what happened to her. "I only gave her a sedative."

Relief washed over him with such force, his knees nearly gave way. "How strong?"

"She'll be out for a while."

"Take her to the cell," he said to the guards holding her.

As they took her away, movement in his peripheral vision made him turn. Three guards approached, jostling Asobo. As the two passed each other, their gazes met. Asobo stopped moving, watching Salma.

India's last word continued to ring in his head.

The guard pushed Salma. "Move it."

Asobo's hands flexed, his nostrils flaring. Anger burned in his eyes. Omar recognised the look. Asobo was in love with Salma. They were in this together. It was the only way Salma could have drugged and tied India without intervention from the guards on duty.

Seeing the man, someone he'd trusted with his and his loved ones' lives, who'd betrayed him in the worst way, produced something feral in him. His own hands flexed, demanding physical release.

The guards shoved Asobo to his knees in front of him. His head of palace security didn't meet his eyes.

"Why?" Omar asked. "What did you lack that you would seek to take so much from me?"

Asobo seemed to have retreated into himself, his expression unreadable. Darkness brewed in Omar, filled him with hatred.

"Did you convince her to do it, or was it the other way around?"

Silence met this question. He swore, his control slipping several notches.

"What did you plan on doing with her? Did you really think you could sneak her out of here without being caught?"

Still not a peep in response. He cursed again.

"Stand," he said, his voice sounding unruffled—the calm before the storm.

Asobo blinked, appearing surprised by the change in tone.

"You declared war by hurting people I love," he continued. "Now, you'll stand before me like a man and fight."

The other man remained on his knees.

"Raise him," he commanded the men who had brought Asobo in.

They did as he asked.

"You want to hurt me, right?" He balled his fists again. "Hands up and fight!"

"You can do anything to me, Sire. I will not fight you," Asobo said.

Rage bourgeoned within him.

"Really?"

He shoved the guy. *This isn't me.* The voice of reason attempted to make an entrance, reminding him he was the diplomat. Brain over brawn. He'd rather talk than hit any day. Every human being had the capacity for rational thinking. That was the mantra he'd lived by most of his adult life, but reason had flown out of the window the moment he'd entered his home and found India on the floor, barely able to keep her eyes open. The fear of losing her had pushed him towards insanity.

With sudden clarity, he realised the only way to reach Asobo was through his heart.

"What about her? Do you care what I can do to her?" he said. "They are taking her to the cells, and I can promise you she won't see the light of day again."

Muscles tightened in Asobo's jaw.

Bingo.

"For her role in this, I'll make her bleed. I'll put her in so much physical pain, she'll beg for death," he spat out. "I won't give her death, though. No. That will be too kind for her crimes."

Asobo's hand twitched. His lips tightened.

"Don't worry. I'll put you in the next cell and make you listen. I'll do unthinkable things to her, touch her in places she hasn't been touched before."

Asobo growled, taking a wide swing. Omar ducked, easily avoiding impact, and delivered a hook that landed squarely on his opponent's jaw. Asobo's next punch caught him in the ribs. The sting felt good, reminded him he was alive; more than he could say for his brother.

Anger blinded him, pumped adrenalin into his body. Adrenalin made him stronger, sharper. He didn't think, only did, as he ducked and swerved, avoiding most of Asobo's incensed punches. Arm-locking his opponent, he landed some blows, then shoving him off, he followed with a series of punches, each one on mark. Asobo fought well, but he was no match for Omar. Though he had military training, too, he lacked Omar's astuteness and the karate black belt.

Asobo stumbled, and Omar's next hook put him back on his knees.

"Get up!"

As he tried to advance, arms wrapped around him. *Weak arms.* He yanked out of them.

"*Tawaquf*, Omar!" His mother's voice cut through his anger, reached down to the humanity hiding beneath. "Stop this madness."

As if he'd been doused with iced water, her voice stole the fight from him, but his body still shook under the weight of emotions. Arms—more arms—wrapped around him. He fought to bring his breathing back to normal as he stared at the faces of his mother, Faridah, and Janae.

"He killed my brother." His throat constricted. "He killed your son, *ya'umi.*"

"The gods allowed it to happen," his mother said. "Will you kill the messenger?"

"If that's what it takes."

His mother's look softened. Her hands touched his face, wiping moisture he hadn't realised was draining from his eyes.

"Look at him, *abnay aleaziz*."

He turned. Asobo remained in the ground, blood trickling from his nose and a cut on his lips.

"*La tuadhiyha, ya malak*." Even now, Asobo pleaded for the woman he had the misfortune of falling for. "Visit her punishment on me, my king."

He tore his eyes from the traitor.

"Take him away," he instructed the guards.

He'd deal with Asobo and Salma later. Now, he needed to get back to India.

***

India's eyes fluttered open. She blinked to clear her vision. Familiar surroundings of their bedroom met her gaze. She winced at the dull ache in her head.

"She's waking up," someone said.

It sounded like Faridah. She turned her head. Omar came into view.

"Hi." He smiled. "We need to stop meeting like this."

"What happened?"

The moment the words came out, everything came rushing back. She gasped.

"Salma! She's the one."

"We got her."

She tried to sit up. "Asobo—"

"We got him, too."

She stared at him, a part of her trying to mentally pinch herself just to make sure she was still alive.

"You're safe," he said. It was a little scary the way he seemed to know her thoughts. "I promise to do a better job of keeping it that way."

She let out a breath, relaxing. *It's over.* "I guess one less thing to accuse Da Silva of."

"Who's Da Silva?" Janae asked.

"How are you feeling?" Queen Azmera asked at the same time.

She decided it best to swerve Janae's question. "I'm fine. A little headache, nothing serious."

The three women came to her side, edging Omar out.

"I'm sorry," she said to them. "If it wasn't for me, Majid would still be alive."

Queen Azmera gave a sad smile and shook her head. "It seems to me it's the other way around. My son started a relationship with Nala Khalid, Salma's sister, when their mother worked here. We discouraged it. Majid was bound to enter a marriage alliance, so any relationship or scandal couldn't have been allowed."

"Majid was stubborn." The sound of King Rafael's voice drew their collective attention to the door. "He wouldn't listen to reason. We made the painful decision of sending the Khalids away."

India absorbed the information. At least, Salma seemed to have told the truth.

"We felt bad for taking their mother's job away, so we made sure to compensate her well," Queen Azmera said.

"Unfortunately, we've learned that their mother died, and they had to return to Sudar," King Rafael continued. "I guess it was just a matter of time before he found her again. I just never realised he was still searching for her."

"Did she say anything to you?" Janae asked.

India nodded and related the gist of what Salma had told her. A moment of silence ensued.

Janae shook her head. "To think we took Majid to be the one with no secrets."

"At least, we know there was a bad boy underneath all that good-boy exterior," Faridah said and earned herself a pointed look from the queen.

The king took her hand. "Majid sinned greatly against you by not being upfront about his relationship with Nala. Can you find it in your heart to forgive him?"

"There's no need for forgiveness, Your Majesty. He can only be accused of being in love." After a moment, she frowned. "What will happen to Nala?"

"We'll make sure she's cared for," Omar spoke from behind his parents.

"We better leave you now," Queen Azmera said. "The doctor said you should take it easy today, but you'll be fine."

India received hugs and handshakes along with well-wishes from them before they filed out, leaving her with Omar. He came to her side, sitting on the bed. He stretched out beside her, propping himself on one elbow. Her body began to tingle as she looked into his eyes.

He cupped her cheek. "I thought I'd lost you, *ya amira*. When I walked in and saw you on the floor, my heart stopped."

"I thought she'd poisoned me." She touched his handsome face. "All I could think about was that I wish I could see your face one more time."

"I can't believe I'm saying this, but it's a good thing they didn't plan a quick death for you."

She knew exactly what he meant. A moment of silence followed while she mused about how badly things could have been.

"I want to show you something," he said and retrieved his phone from the bedside unit behind him. He swiped and executed a few taps, then held the screen up to her.

Her eyes widened as she gazed at the image displayed.

"Sophia?"

"Look at the time stamp."

She checked a series of numbers at the bottom right of the photo. "That's today's date."

"Shaka has eyes on the ground. He assures me she's safe, and she'll be watched twenty-four-seven until she's rescued." After returning the phone where he'd picked it from, he added, "If Da Silva makes the mistake of hurting her in any way, I promise you I'll make him pay."

Her heart squeezed into a tight ball. "I love you, Omar."

"I know." He stared at her for several seconds. "Thank you."

She frowned "For what?"

"For finally saying it.

"Finally?"

"I saw it in your eyes when we made love, heard it in your voice when you said my name. I dared to hope it was real." He brushed her face with the tips of his fingers. A shudder passed through her. "It pleases me to hear it on your lips."

"That first day, I felt it, too," she confessed. "I told myself I'd imagined it, but when I woke up in the hospital bed, you kissed my face, and I knew I'd been lying to myself."

The corners of his lips curved up in a slow, sexy smile. "Still, you decided to torture me."

She shrugged. "You did accuse me of treason."

He raised his brows in mock concentration. "That is true."

She giggled. When he kissed her again, his passion swept her, melting her insides. She gave herself over to the kiss, allowing his essence to feed her, body and soul. This was where she wanted to be. Always.

"I love you, India. You are and will always be the only one for me," he said after they parted. "Marry me."

"We're already married."

"Then marry me again, *ya omri*, with your consent this time."

Tears prickled her eyes, and she nodded. "I consent to marrying you, Omar. *Ana Bahebik, ya malik.*"

He blinked. "Your diction is impeccable."

"I have a knack for languages."

"Is that so? What other talents do you have?"

She grinned. "You'll find out in the course of our marriage."

"Intriguing." His right hand, which had been caressing her abdomen, moved up to cup her breast. Her breathing accelerated as he teased her nipple into a hard peak.

"Didn't the doctor say to take it easy?" she said, even though she shifted closer.

Unperturbed, his hand moved to seek the wetness between her thighs. "Then you're going to have to be very still."

A cry left her lips as he found one of her sensitive spots and concentrated there. Joy swelled in her heart while pleasure spread its tentacles through her. She pulled his head down, and kissed him, giving herself over to his ministrations.

This was where she belonged, where she was always meant to be. In Omar's arms.

CHAPTER EIGHTEEN

African ROYALS Unlimited Online

OMAR EL DANSURI BECOMES NEW KING OF SUDAR

Story Highlights

Omar and wife, Princess India, crowned King and Queen at their first official ceremony

Omar became India's husband through wife inheritance custom of Sudar

King Rafael signed his abdication into law at midnight after 40-year reign, announced move last month, citing ill-health.

There were no ritzy official celebrations, kingdom still in mourning after death of older brother, Majid.

Omar given military sash at palace, addressed citizens in a televised press event, joined by wife to wave from balcony

Streets of M'Bamina lined with Sudari flags ready for new king and queen.

Uncle, Sheikh Latif, side-lined from events after being found guilty of treason, son takes over as Emir of Umm Jafar

The new king was crowned in a low-key ceremony held in the Royal Council Chamber of the Sultan's Castle, M'Bamina, witnessed by family and key members of the royal court.

Omar takes over from his father Rafael who signed his abdication papers at midnight, ending a forty-year reign as absolute monarch of the small African kingdom. He was propelled into the position of heir apparent following the death of his brother, Majid, in a car accident nearly a month ago on his way to his honeymoon with new bride, Princess India of Bagumi.

The new queen became Omar's wife following a wife inheritance ceremony performed in accordance with Sudari customs. India, the daughter of King Ibrahim Saene of Bagumi, married into the Sudar royal family to seal an alliance between the two African kingdoms.

Staying within the sombreness of the mourning period still being observed in Sudar, the new monarch and his wife were conveyed through M'Bamina in a subdued affair after a brief military parade to their first official engagement.

Later, a reception for five-hundred guests at the royal palace featured finger foods, several notches below the elaborate banquet that had been planned for his brother's coronation, a deliberate act to acknowledge the grief that is still raw in many Sudari hearts.

Absent from the event was Omar's uncle, Latif, who has been put under house arrest after being charged with treason, details of which have not been released to the public. His son, Faruk, takes over as Emir of the semi-autonomous state of Umm Jafar.

Sudar is one of the last absolute monarchies in the world, a kingdom with deep-seated traditions dating back hundreds of years. In his address to the nation, Omar reflected on the country's economic situation, urging his citizens to embrace change as the means to meet the challenges of a globalised world.

He emphasised the importance of women in his vision of a better Sudar, and in an unprecedented move, announced the appointment of his sister, Faridah, as Minister of Culture and Tourism. This position puts the Sudari princess at the forefront of the promised reforms.

Following his first official address, the new king and queen stood on the balcony and waved to well-wishers. As Omar and India gazed at each other with obvious love, it was clear that this marriage alliance has bloomed into love. Their first public kiss sparked excitement and anticipation (and if we're being honest, bets) for the arrival of a royal baby sooner rather than later.

Thank you for reading His Inherited Princess. Carry on reading to find out more about the next book in the Royal House of Saene series.

BLURB: His Captive Princess by Kiru Taye

Isha Saene has perfected the act of balancing her life—a celebrated corporate negotiator spearheading an international trade deal that could catapult her country to one of the fastest growing mid-sized economies in Africa, and a loyal First Princess of Bagumi Kingdom set to seal ties with a neighbouring nation through marriage.

Until one careless moment knocks her carefully choreographed life into chaos.

Zain Bassong has always fought for the underdog—a patriot dedicated to fighting against the oppression of his people by the country's elite. He believes the pen is mightier than the sword and chooses the diplomatic route, no matter how many times he is arrested by the repressive regime.

Until devastating news triggers a chain reaction.

Isha and Zain are thrown together and their lives change. For better or worse? They will have to figure that out before it's too late.

EXCERPT: His Captive Princess by Kiru Taye

"Mr Bassong, if you will, please arrange for a phone to be sent to me. I would like to rest now. You are dismissed."

He burst out laughing, a cold, echoing mirth that didn't reach his eyes and chilled her to the bones.

As quickly as it started the laughter died and he took a step in her direction.

Her impulse was to step back but she hadn't done anything impulsive in years. She stayed where she stood as he advanced.

"First Princess Isha Ruby—"

"Don't call me that!" Isha couldn't stop the visceral response or the vehemence in her voice when he used her middle name. Her gut wrenched and the throbbing returned to her temple.

He jerked back and raised one dark brow.

"Is that not your name, Ruby Bagumi?" The tone of his voice baited her and his rigid posture mocked her.

She stiffened her spine and squared her shoulders. "You know very well that I am the First Princess of Bagumi Kingdom and my given name is Isha Saene. You can address me as Your Highness or Princess Isha."

"Oh." He tilted his head and scratched the hair on his chin. "Ten years ago, I met a student in London. She was beautiful, intelligent, compassionate, or at least I'd thought she was at the time. She had these brilliant ideas that could change the world. She told me her name was Ruby Bagumi. But I found out it was a lie."

He cut her open with his words, a thousand papercuts, making her bleed from her soul.

She closed her eyes tight and balled her fists.

She would not go there, would not bleed for him to see.

I am First Princess Isha Saene, she recited in her mind. Isha Saene.

"I am First Princess Isha Saene," she said out loud and took a deep breath as she opened her eyes.

He stood close. If she reached out she could place her palm on this chest. Was his heart thumping as hard as hers? His scent clung in the air, sandalwood and citrus, tantalising her with each breath.

Memories she'd locked away hovered, threatening to break free.

Nails biting into her palms, she took a step back. "I demand a phone call."

"So that's the way you want to play it." He nodded, moving away as he made his proclamation. "First Princess Isha Saene of the Kingdom of Bagumi, you are now a captive of the MLG group. You will remain in our custody until our demands are met. As for your demand—" he spat out the word as if it was offensive "—you have no power and no rights here. This is Wanai where the supreme power remains with the supreme leader and in this region, I am the supreme leader. You will do as you are told while you are here."

"I will not," she retorted, bristling that he dared to make such a declaration. "I do not submit to your leadership. The only authorities I recognise are my father, His Majesty the King of Bagumi and Almighty God."

He gave that cold laughter again, the one that sent shivers down her spine.

"You are engaged to a Wanaian man. What do you think will happen after you are wedded? In Wanai, your husband will have total authority over you."

Her chin jutted as she glared at him. "Kweku and anyone else will be out of their freaking minds if they think I'm going to abide by that antiquated edict."

Her mother would blanch in horror if she had heard Isha speak in this manner. Language suited only to commoners. Still, this man made her forget herself and her upbringing every time.

"There she is. There is the woman I once knew as Ruby Bagumi." For the first time, a small smile tugged the corner of his lips. "Welcome to Wanai. Make yourself comfortable, well, as comfortable as you can under the circumstances. I'll see you again soon."

He whirled around and was gone before she could respond.

Her chest heaved as she tried to catch her breath and make sense of what just happened.

Why was Zain doing this to her? Why was he set on resurrecting the past?

OTHER BOOKS BY LOVE AFRICA PRESS

Healing His Medic by Nana Prah

Queer and Sexy Collection Volume 1 by Eniitan

His Defiant Princess by Nana Prah

His Captive Princess by Kiru Taye

Bound To Liberty by Kiru Taye

CONNECT WITH US

Facebook.com/LoveAfricaPress

Twitter.com/LoveAfricaPress

Instagram.com/LoveAfricaPress

www.loveafricapress.com

www.ingramcontent.com/pod-product-compliance
Lightning Source LLC
Chambersburg PA
CBHW050848190726
48286CB00007B/2274